NO OTHER LOVE

A Walker Island Romance, Book 2

Lucy Kevin

NO OTHER LOVE
A Walker Island Romance, Book 2

Come for a visit to Walker Island where you'll find stunning Pacific Northwest ocean views, men too intriguing to resist...and five beautiful, close-knit sisters who are each about to find their one true love.

Morgan Walker, makeup artist to the stars, never thought she'd leave New York City to come back to Walker Island. But when she is tapped to headline her own TV makeover show, she decides it's the perfect time to launch her organic makeup line made from flowers and plants grown on the Walker family plot of land. While she's really excited about getting to spend a few weeks with the sisters and grandmother she doesn't see nearly often enough, she's equally worried about the possibility of seeing Brian Russell again. Because even though they broke up seven years ago, she's never been able to forget him. Not for one single day...

When Brian gets the opportunity to work with Morgan on planting her new garden, he immediately jumps at it. Seven years ago, he thought he was doing the right thing by letting her go to pursue her dreams and see the world. But he's never stopped loving her, and now that she's finally back, he's determined to do whatever it takes to convince her that they belong together...forever this time.

CHAPTER ONE

"Oh my gosh, you're Morgan Walker! Can we take a picture with you?"

Morgan had been up at 4 a.m. in her New York City apartment, quickly eating half of a bagel and drinking a cup of scalding coffee before heading out to Times Square to shoot her makeup segment on the morning news show. Shooting had, inevitably, gone longer than scheduled, which always seemed to happen when she needed to catch a plane or train. After a taxi ride through bumper-to-bumper traffic to the airport, a six-hour flight to Seattle, where even her legendary napping abilities had been challenged by noisy fellow passengers, another long taxi trip down to the harbor, and then this ferry ride, Morgan was looking forward to dropping straight into bed when she finally got to her family's home. But after dreaming her whole life of being a successful makeup artist, she would never complain when people recognized her.

"Absolutely," she said with a smile for the two teenage girls who were looking at her with stars in their eyes. After they posed for the girl's father, who was taking the pictures, she asked, "Are you going to Walker Island for vacation?"

"We are," the teen with the cropped red hair said, "but we're worried it is going to be *so* boring to be stuck on an island for a whole week. Is there *anything* to do there?"

Morgan smiled, remembering what it was like to be fourteen and feeling like Walker Island was the smallest, sleepiest, most unimportant place in the world. All she'd wanted was to get out and see the world and experience *everything.* And it was exactly what she'd done. What she was still doing, actually, apart from the next few weeks when she'd be working on the island to launch her own organic makeup line before heading back to New York.

But she didn't want the girls to feel bad about their upcoming vacation, so she told them, "Actually, there's quite a bit to do on the island. Kayaking. Rock climbing. Snorkeling. Painting. Dancing. There's some pretty good shopping on the island, too." As the long list continued to fall rather easily from her lips, Morgan was more than a little surprised. Had there always been so much to do on the island? Granted, plenty of new businesses had popped up over the years as island living had come more and more into vogue.

Thankfully, both girls now looked a little less depressed about the idea of spending their vacation on an island as one of them asked, "Did you really grow up here?"

"I did." And for all that she'd longed to get off of the island as soon as she was old enough to escape to the city, now she found sweet memories of growing up on the island slipping through her mind, one after the other. All the times she'd "camped" in the backyard with her sisters as a kid, sitting around making s'mores, then going back inside to her own bed when it got dark enough to scare even Emily. The bonfires down at the caves when she was a teenager, where the local teens would have parties most weekends. And best of all, snuggling up beside Brian Russell on the beach as they watched the whales swim by—

Forcing herself to stop that train of thought as quickly as it had formed in her head, she said, "The island is small and pretty remote, but my family is really great, and I had lots of good friends, too, so it was actually a pretty great place to grow up."

"But don't you live in New York City now? That must be awesome!"

Again, she nodded. "It's fun living and working in the city." But sometimes—a lot of times, if she was being completely honest—she wished that she had family there. Or some *really* good friends, rather than a group of people with whom she enjoyed going out on the town to Broadway shows and the newest, hippest restaurants, but to whom she couldn't quite imagine spilling her deepest secrets.

"Girls," their father said, "we should leave Ms. Walker alone now."

Though she let him know she was enjoying their conversation, the girls were already busy posting the pictures online, and soon Morgan was standing alone again on the Walker Island ferry's deck. Turning back to the water, she breathed in the salty air and let the brisk wind blow her blond hair back from her face as seagulls flew and swooped all around the ferry.

The ping of a text coming through on her cell phone snapped Morgan out of her near-doze against the rail of the ferry, and she quickly scanned the message from her assistant, Juliet, who had the fastest texting thumbs Morgan had ever seen.

Hope your trip to the island was good. Having some problems with one of the new island interns. Claims he can't miss football practice at 5!

Not nearly as proficient at texting, Morgan decided to call instead of typing out a message back.

"Hi, boss." Juliet had the ultra-professional PA thing down perfectly when it was needed, which

Morgan greatly appreciated, but she was also glad that Juliet could be easygoing when it was just the two of them. Much like Morgan's oldest sister, Emily, who was incredibly organized and focused, but still knew how to relax and hang out when it was just family. "How do you want me to deal with the slacker intern?"

Morgan laughed. "Football is a bit of a religion on the island, so why don't we simply move the meeting with the interns up to four p.m.? That should solve the problem. And I wasn't planning anything important for this afternoon, anyway." Except for a really delicious nap, but clearly napping wasn't in the cards for her today.

"I always forget that you're not a native New Yorker until you go back home for a visit, and we end up having to rearrange your schedule around football practice and whale-watching tours," Juliet remarked. "In any case, I will let you know immediately if anything comes through on the revised contract details for your new makeup line."

After they concluded the call and Morgan slipped her phone back into her bright red Kate Spade carryall, it struck her how different her upbringing had been from her assistant's. Juliet had gone to an exclusive all-girls private school on the East Coast, so it was no wonder that she didn't have an insight into the importance of Walker High's football team to the island community. Trying to change the practice schedule would have been like trying to move the planet out of its orbit. And would probably also earn her a talking-to from Emily, if not from their father, both of whom worked for the local school. Emily was the guidance counselor, and Tres was the English teacher who was frequently in Europe during the summer leading literary tours for local teenagers.

A few minutes later, Morgan stepped from the ferry onto the dock. Though she had been back only a month ago for her sister Hanna's wedding to Joel Peterson, Morgan took a few moments to look around at the waterfront. Things on Walker Island, she thought as she looked around her at the boathouse and the bakery and little grocery store that had been there ever since she was a kid, so rarely changed. And while that had often been frustrating for her as a teenager, now that she was an adult, she found that she was glad for the permanency of it—for knowing that there was a solid foundation, and community, that she could always count on being there. No matter what.

She was especially glad that seven decades after her grandfather, William II, had sold the berry-picking business, the Walker family still kept a small, one-acre plot of land in the center of the island. It was that land that had inspired Morgan's new business plan and this trip back home.

As soon as the network had offered Morgan

her own thirty-minute makeover show, she had decided it was the perfect time to launch her own makeup line. And because it would need to stand out from the lines that much bigger celebrities brought out seemingly every week, what could be better than the story of heading home to grow the organic ingredients from her family's historic farmland with the help of the local high school students and community?

Plus, after so many years away working around the clock, she'd begun to miss her family more and more. She hoped that growing some of the ingredients for her makeup line on the island would give her plenty of opportunities to come back more often. And if she happened to see Brian from time to time...well, she'd just have to figure out a way to keep whatever feelings had remained for him inside. Because if there was one thing she knew with absolute certainty, it was how terribly painful it was to let yourself fall in love with someone when you knew from the start that you could never end up together.

Morgan wasn't sure what Brian was doing these days, although admittedly it had taken a pretty big effort on her part not to ask her sisters for updates or to poke around on Facebook to see how his life had turned out since high school. Still, if he'd gotten married, she was absolutely sure someone would have called to mention it. Whether he had a girlfriend, on the other hand...

Morgan gave her head a quick shake. She

should be happy for him if he did have a girlfriend, because it would mean he had gotten on with his life, just like she'd gotten on with hers. Because she *had* gotten on with it, hadn't she? Even if she didn't have a boyfriend in New York and had never felt many sparks fly with any of the men she'd dated in the city, well, it was probably just because she worked such long hours and was often too tired for all the small talk and flirting.

"Ms. Walker?" One of the staff who worked on the docks came up to her. "Your rental car is waiting for you in the lot at the far end of the dock." The man handed over a set of keys.

Morgan thanked him, but as she stared at the keys in her hand, she couldn't help but wonder what he must be thinking. Maybe that since she'd left the island, she'd become such a big star in her own mind that she couldn't manage the short walk to her family's home? The truth was, Juliet never seemed to remember just how small the island was, so of course she'd arranged transportation. Morgan knew she should be thankful that it wasn't a limo with a driver, because she *never* would have lived that one down...

The sleek red convertible waiting for her seemed to scream, *I'm on TV!* Clearly, she should have done a better job of explaining to Juliet how things worked on Walker Island, with everything stopping for football practice, artists wandering around with easels under their arms, and marine biologists making up a shifting population of well-educated drifters. All the little things that were so normal and wonderful to Morgan because she'd grown up a Pacific Northwest island girl. Of course, as she slid in behind the steering wheel onto the soft leather seats and the engine started with a soft purr, she had to admit that the convertible did suit the part of her that loved beautiful, luxurious things built for speed.

These were the two sides of her that had always clashed and that she'd never quite been able to reconcile: the girl who loved the beauty and serenity of the island and the woman who thrived in a big city as a makeup artist.

Morgan had been thirteen years old when Grams had passed her the makeup bag before one of her dance school's productions of *Swan Lake* and said, "You're better with makeup than I am, dear. Will you take over?"

Morgan could still remember how much fun she'd had that night. She'd never been able to dance as beautifully as Paige could, but she'd done a fabulous job of turning her sister into the black swan, disguising her natural features so well that people had commented on the makeup almost as much as Paige's excellent dancing.

It was strange, Morgan found herself thinking, that a career that had led to a national TV slot could start so simply. Or that she would find herself back on Walker Island about to embark on the biggest challenge of her life.

Almost as if coming home had always been inevitable...

CHAPTER TWO

Before Morgan stepped into the school's main hallway, she quickly reread her intern's résumés on her phone. She'd gone over them months ago when her sister Emily had sent them over from the school, but between Morgan's busy shooting schedule and negotiations on her makeup line and TV show, she hadn't had a chance to refresh her memory.

Their grandfather had built the Walker Island school in the 1950s, and it had always felt like a second home to Morgan and her sisters, who had often curled up in the soft chair in their father's office while he graded English papers or worked on planning another school trip. Even now, he was away for a few more weeks with his students, showing them the important literary sites around Europe.

She looked down the long lines of lockers,

easily imagining students running off to their classes before the final bell rang. The nearest set looked the same as they had when she had been a student, right down to the stickers the janitor still hadn't been able to peel off. Again, Morgan found memories moving up through her, the past coming back all too easily. Particularly that night when she and Brian had snuck away from the senior prom, not waiting for the announcement of prom king and queen. It just hadn't seemed important. Not when all she wanted was to be alone with him, especially when she'd known how close they were to saying good-bye to each other. He belonged on the island and would clearly never be as happy anywhere else, but she knew she'd never truly be happy if she *didn't* leave and find out what else there was in the world for her.

Even love hadn't been able to change that.

Still, though their relationship had been doomed from the start, Morgan could remember how much time she'd always spent getting ready for school as a teenage girl, fixing her makeup, making sure she looked just right for him. Brian, on the other hand, hadn't had to do anything to look just right. Athletic and tanned with sandy blond hair and a gorgeous smile, he always looked great.

If she closed her eyes, Morgan could almost hear the strains of *You and Me* by Lifehouse playing in the background, just as it had when they had left the prom that night. The lyrics had seemed like they had been written for her and Brian—two people who couldn't keep their eyes off of each other, who felt like their hearts were spinning around and around whenever they kissed.

Morgan could still remember everything about that night, right down to the decorations they'd used on prom night, a combination of vines and wild flowers that Morgan had helped to grow on the Walker acre of land. It had probably been so cheesy, but at the time it had seemed simply beautiful.

Just like the moment when Brian had pulled her into this space between the lockers and kissed her. Even after all these years, Morgan could still remember the instant that their lips had met. It hadn't been even close to their first kiss, but it was the one she always remembered when she thought about him. He had reached up to the decorations, breaking off a small section of flower-covered vine, twisting it into a circlet that he had settled onto her head. His own version of the prom queen's crown. It had been such a simple thing to do. So perfect for the moment. So Brian.

"Forget the prom, Morgan. What matters is that you'll always be my queen."

"Always?" Even after I'm gone? *she'd thought, but she hadn't wanted to ruin everything by saying it aloud. Not when it would happen all too soon.*

But he hadn't paused, hadn't had to think about his answer. He'd simply said, "Always," and then kissed her again, both of them pouring their entire hearts and souls into the kiss. One that they both knew would be one of their very last.

She had never wanted to hurt him, had even tried early on in high school to keep her distance in the hopes of avoiding an inevitable breakup when her dreams to see more of the world eventually overshadowed everything else. But in that moment on prom night in his arms, all she'd wanted for a few precious seconds was to live the dream where she was his, he was hers, and everything was simple. Where it was so easy to be young and in love and no one had to make hard choices.

She sighed, knowing that for all she'd tried over the past seven years to tell herself that she didn't have any regrets about leaving the island—and Brian—coming back to the places that were special to them made it *really* hard to keep believing she wasn't lying to herself.

She wondered what Brian looked like now. Probably as gorgeous as ever, she mused with a pang in the center of her chest.

Two figures came around the corner toward her. Morgan assumed the dark-haired girl was Natalie Fields. She was wearing glasses, carrying a folder and managing to look about as serious as was possible for a seventeen-year-old girl to look. Morgan had asked Emily to recruit kids with an interest in science on the basis that a lot of makeup production was chemistry and the horticulture involved in gathering the ingredients would involve plenty of knowledge of biology.

Natalie certainly fit the bill, and her internship application and high school achievements made it sound like she was a future Marie Curie in the making. Not only was she a straight-A student, but she'd also taken extra-credit biology and had written a very well-researched paper on environmental gardens. With luck, that would make her the perfect assistant when it came to helping to design and cultivate the old Walker plot for the project. The only question mark Morgan could think of was whether the girl would mind leaving the classroom and getting her hands dirty in the garden.

The boy walking beside Natalie was at least a foot taller, with youthful, good-looking features and his hair cut short. Clearly, Tad Burrows was going to be a great help in the brawn department as they farmed the garden. Emily had told her that Tad was the football team's star kicker. His grades, while far from awful, weren't exactly in Natalie's league, which made him a little hard to figure out. For Natalie, being Morgan's intern made perfect sense. It showed colleges that she was serious about a scientific career, gave her experience to bring to employers, and helped her to make contacts in the makeup world if that was what she wanted to go into later. Tad, on the other hand, had clearly been focusing on football so that he could get an athletics scholarship. Nothing in his application suggested that he had any previous interest in gardening or science.

She was about to say hello and introduce herself when a third figure came walking around the corner...and Morgan's breath caught in her throat.

She'd been wrong. Brian wasn't as gorgeous as ever. He was *better* looking than he had been before. He still had the muscular poise of an athlete, and his hair still fell in that unruly, boyish mess, but his features were more rugged now with a wiser, and definitely more confident, edge to his appearance.

For several seconds, Morgan couldn't manage to do anything but stare at him. She could have looked into those deep-blue eyes practically forever, and judging by the way that Brian was looking back at her—

Natalie moved to stand right in front of Morgan and thrust a hand out at her. "It's *such* a pleasure to meet you, Ms. Walker. I've been looking forward to the chance to work with you ever since I heard about the opportunity. I watch your segment on TV whenever it comes on, and I just *loved* what you did with the makeup on that zombie movie you did last year. I mean, the way you made them look half-dead and really *good* all at the same time was amazing, and I'm just in awe of you and all that you've accomplished so far."

Tad shook her hand, too. "Thanks so much for this opportunity, Ms. Walker. We're really excited about working with you. Aren't we, Coach Russell?"

Brian finally smiled at her, and for all that he'd changed, it was exactly the smile Morgan remembered. One that melted her from the inside out.

"It's good to see you again, Morgan."

"It's nice to see you again, too, Brian."

Just that quickly, seven years disappeared as sparks jumped between them again. Sparks that were even hotter and wilder than they had been before.

CHAPTER THREE

My God, Morgan was beautiful.

Morgan had been a pretty girl, but now she was every inch a stunning woman. More worldly. More confident. Wearing designer clothes, her gorgeous blond locks styled into glossy perfection.

But despite those changes, it was her eyes that struck him most. There was still the same restlessness there. The same need to find something bigger. Something *more*. It was one of the things he'd loved about her...even though he'd also known that one day it would be precisely what would pull them apart.

"Are there any celebrities who look, well, normal without their makeup on?" Natalie was asking Morgan as they stepped into Brian's office.

Morgan laughed. "I can't name any names, but yes, there definitely are. Most of the time, the image you see is just the finished product, one that takes quite a lot of time and professionals to create."

"Who's the most famous person you've worked with?" Tad asked next.

Morgan looked a little tired, Brian thought, even though she was answering the kids' questions brightly enough. He had always been able to spot the fatigue in her movements, the slight darkness under her eyes. Obviously, she hadn't managed to snatch one of the afternoon naps she'd always loved so much when they were kids. Morgan had been able to fall asleep almost anywhere. She'd fallen asleep in the library when they were supposed to be studying, in classes when no one was watching, even occasionally in the corner at a party. Once during a family picnic when all of the other Walkers had been bustling around, Morgan had fallen asleep beneath a corner of the red-checkered tablecloth. Her sisters had liked to joke that she had to be part cat to curl up and sleep anywhere like that.

He'd always thought that they'd been right. After all, Morgan was not only beautiful, graceful and tender...she was also far too fiercely independent to ever want to remain in one spot for very long.

"There's something I don't totally get," Tad said. "How did *you* get to be famous when you're just doing makeup for other people?"

"Tad!" Natalie exclaimed. "Ms. Walker does

amazing work, not just with normal people like you and me, but with stars, too. She's the best in the business!"

"I know that," Tad said, his face turning a little red as he belatedly realized he'd put his foot in his mouth. Especially in front of the girl that he clearly had a major crush on. "I just don't understand—"

"How that translates to fame?" Morgan finished for him. "I'm not sure I understand it myself, some days." She laughed again, and the sound warmed every part of Brian that had been cold for the past seven years. "I was very much in the background as a makeup artist until I started doing the TV makeover segments and a few of my online how-to videos went viral. I'm just glad it *did* end up working out like that, though, or I might not have such a good job now."

But was she truly glad that she was famous now? Because as they headed through to Brian's office, maybe most other people wouldn't have seen it—it was obvious that neither Natalie nor Tad did—but being the focus of their awestruck questions was obviously making Morgan uncomfortable. There was that note of tension under the surface that Brian had always been able to spot. Morgan was doing her best to answer the kids' questions, but it seemed to him that having to play the celebrity wasn't quite as easy for Morgan as it would have been for someone who had truly been chasing fame rather than adventure.

Brian could remember that look well, the way she'd closed up a little bit every time someone had made a big deal about her being a Walker when they were kids. From the “I know your sisters” comments, to the looks she got from those on the Peterson side of the old island feud, to the tourists who had treated her as if she were one of the island’s attractions.

But then, maybe the difference with her fame as a makeup artist was that it came out of doing what she loved, whereas the Walker family fame simply lumped her together with her sisters and tied her down to the past. And Brian knew as well as anyone how little Morgan liked being tied down.

“Nice office,” Morgan said, looking around the small space that Brian occupied when he wasn’t in a classroom or out on the field coaching. It was a little disorganized at the moment with stacks of books along one wall, football plays written up on a board at one side, and enough assorted piles of paper on his desk that it was hard to see the wood beneath. “It's great that you're the football coach,” Morgan added while Natalie and Tad found space to sit.

“I also teach science,” Brian explained, since she had to be wondering why he was involved with her interns. “Your internship falls under the science department, and since one of our interns is also a football player, I was the obvious point of contact for you on this."

Actually, he'd volunteered for it. Not that anyone else on staff seemed to mind. Even Morgan's sister had been surprisingly okay with it. Probably because she knew how interested Brian was in seeing Morgan again. After all, her sisters had been almost as upset as he was when Morgan left the island immediately after graduating high school.

"Mr. Russell is the best science teacher *ever*," Natalie said with the same enthusiasm she'd used greeting Morgan. "I've learned so much in his classes."

"Students like Natalie make it very easy for me to do my job," Brian said. It sounded like the kind of thing a teacher was expected to say, but really, it was the truth. Odds were that, with or without his help, Natalie would eventually work her way into the top echelons of science. In fact, Brian wouldn't be too surprised if, twenty years from now, she was picking up the Nobel Prize for some discovery. She was the kind of kid who seemed to live inside her books and her brilliant mind. All Brian had to do was point her in the right direction from time to time. One really good thing about this internship was that he hoped it might coax her out of the library once in a while.

Tad...well, he was a little more work. Tad was a smart kid, but he definitely wasn't the kind of student Brian would ordinarily have expected to get involved with a project like this. That his star kicker had signed up said quite a lot about just how big his crush on Natalie was. Especially since his eyes hadn't left the girl's face since they'd come into the office.

Brian wasn't sure if Natalie had even noticed that Tad was interested in her when practically any other girl in the school would have jumped at the chance to go out with the football team's star. Clearly, Tad didn't believe in making life easy for himself, either with the internship or with his crush.

Funny, Brian thought, it was a lot like how he'd always felt around Morgan. Because instead of falling for one of the island girls who had no urge whatsoever to leave for the city, he'd willingly given his heart to her when they were kids.

And now, seven years since he'd last seen her, one look was all it had taken for him to realize that he was just as head over heels in love with Morgan as he'd been back in high school.

"Brian?" Morgan began to reach for him, but pulled her hand back at the last moment. "Is everything okay?"

Knowing the last thing he could do in front of his students was blurt out his love for her, he nodded and said, "Your assistant sent over some waivers for everyone to sign." He rooted through his stacks of paperwork until he found them. "We also have one for you about not holding the school liable for anything to do with the project, along with the state education forms to make the internships official for Natalie's and Tad's transcripts."

"Wait a minute," Morgan said as she frowned at the school's internship forms. "It says here that the supervisor must be present on all excursions." She looked up at him, her eyes such a beautiful blue that he needed to grab on to the desk to steady himself. "Are you really planning to be with the three of us every single time we work together on my project?"

"I think the idea is to have some supervision for the students, make sure everything's going okay, and have some continuity with my science class." Brian worked to make the plan sound as natural—and as casual—as he could. "Plus, in the event that something were to go wrong, I will be able to step in and help out immediately. Not that I think anything's going to go wrong, obviously."

Morgan pressed her lips together at that, and Brian couldn't help remembering the sweet yet sinful sensation of them against his own. Her lips had tasted so delicious every time they'd kissed, the flavor of her lip gloss changing as often as her mood. She'd treated makeup as a means of self-expression, the way someone else might use paint or music. She had always been an artist, one with really, really beautiful lips that he'd dreamed of kissing again for seven long years...

Somehow, Brian managed to turn his focus back to the papers they each needed to sign and the schedule his students needed to keep to fit in all of their activities. "Practice starts in five minutes, Tad. You should probably head out now that the contracts are signed."

Tad looked a little startled by the reminder. He'd obviously been watching Natalie instead of the clock. He really had it bad.

Brian knew exactly how he felt.

"Thanks for the reminder, Coach. And thanks again for this opportunity, Ms. Walker." He turned to the girl beside him, wearing his heart entirely on his sleeve. "Bye, Natalie."

After giving him a friendly wave, Natalie told them, "I need to go, too, unfortunately. I've got an experiment running in the science lab." Clearly, she wished she could stay to produce Morgan's entire makeup line right there and then.

"When we have more time together," Morgan said, "I'd love to hear more about what you're working on at school."

The girl looked thrilled. "Oh my gosh, I would *love* to talk to you about things. Anything, really, since you've seen and done so much."

And then, for the first time in seven incredibly long years, Brian and Morgan were alone together again.

"Don't you have to head out to the football field, too?" Morgan asked.

"Nope, one of the assistant coaches is running today's practice."

Brian racked his brain to think of *something*

he could say to Morgan that would get her to stay, even just a few minutes longer. But standing this close to her muddled up his brain and turned it to mush. Just the way her kisses always had.

But Morgan wasn't turning to leave. Instead, she was looking at him with an expression on her face that he couldn't quite read. "Do you want to go and get a drink?"

Her question was so sudden that it took Brian completely by surprise. It was the very last thing he'd been expecting.

And the very best.

"I'd love to."

CHAPTER FOUR

As they walked the short distance to the local hangout on Main Street, Morgan tried to think of things they could talk about that wouldn't end up circling back to their teenage romantic relationship. She hadn't intended to ask Brian to have a drink with her, but once the papers had been signed and the kids had walked away, she'd realized she wasn't ready to walk away from him. Not yet. Not when he looked and smelled so good. Not when his smile was so sweet and so sexy.

And not when she'd finally realized just how much she'd missed him all these years.

Given that they were going to be working alongside one another every single day for the next several weeks, she had spontaneously decided that the best thing they could do was go for a friendly drink to show that they could get along without their past getting in the way. A simple “I’m not pining over you and you’re not pining over me” drink. It was the right thing to do. The adult thing to do. After all, they weren’t hormone-driven, angst-ridden kids anymore.

They walked in silence for a couple of minutes before they reached the Seaman’s Pub. It was mostly full of locals and the marine biology crowd, who came over to do research on the whales and the waters around the island, and played up the maritime image with nets and pictures of the island’s whale “regulars” on the walls. It was strange to think that she and Brian had been eighteen the last time they'd gone out together and hadn't been old enough to set foot inside the pub.

“How is your mother doing?” Morgan asked.

“She’s great now, completely over her illness. She’s living in Seattle now and loves being in the city.”

“So she's happy?” Morgan had always liked Brian’s mother and had been really sad when she'd gotten sick midway through their high school years. Brian had always done such a good job of taking care of his mom that it had been just one more reason to love him. At the same time, she was surprised to hear that Mrs. Russell wasn't on the island anymore, because that meant that Brian was living here without any family at all.

“She's very happy, actually. My dad and I were the big island lovers, not her.” He looked at

Morgan, and in his eyes she read his acceptance of that fact. Just the way he'd always accepted it about *her.*

Brian bought them drinks while she looked for a table. She tried to find a spot where they'd have plenty of space, but after he returned with the drinks she quickly realized that due to a couple of biologists who were loudly discussing approaches to underwater photography at the next table, they would have to sit quite close to each other if they wanted to actually be able to hear each other talk.

"How have the makeover segments been going?"

"Really well," Morgan said. "Especially when I'm working with someone who is on the verge of making a big change in their life and I can see what a difference the makeover makes to them. That's when it feels like I've done something really great." There weren't many men who she believed would understand that, but Brian had always understood more than anyone else. And despite their years apart, something told her he still did.

"I loved that makeover you did awhile back in Idaho when you helped the girl get ready for her prom."

Maybe Morgan should have been surprised that Brian's favorite makeover segment was the same as her own, but she wasn't. Not when they'd always been able to finish each other's sentences—and thoughts. Truly, the only thing that *did* surprise her was that Brian watched her on TV at all. Clearly, he hadn't been nearly as intent on blocking her out of his life these past seven years as she had with him. It was just that it had hurt so much every time she thought about him...

Belatedly realizing he was waiting for her to respond, she said, "I loved working with Charlene. Not just making her beautiful for her big night, but convincing her that she *is* beautiful, wheelchair and all."

"Everything about that segment really felt like you," Brian said, shifting closer to Morgan as another loud crew of biologists came into the bar. "Particularly being out on the road and watching you explore the new town with Charlene as your guide. I know how much you love to see new places and experience new things." He smiled at her again, that warm, heart-melting smile. "You're so good at what you do that I wouldn't be surprised if the network offers you your own show soon."

After the way things had ended between them, Morgan was amazed that he could be so sweet and supportive about her career. But, then, Brian had always been a wonderful man. One who had loved her with his whole heart and had never played games. Not even when he knew that she was leaving for sure right after graduation. He hadn't tried to get in her way, hadn't tried to hold her back. She'd loved him so much for that...even as an irrational part of her had been so disappointed that he'd just let her go.

"Actually, we are wrapping up negotiations to expand my segment into my own show."

His huge grin made her heartbeat kick up even faster inside her chest. "That's great news, Morgan. You've always blown me away."

Flustered by the intense way he was looking at her, and the incredibly sweet things he was saying, Morgan had to work really hard to keep the heat from her cheeks as she asked, "What about you? I'm guessing that you must love coaching the football team."

"I do love it. Not just the winning, though I'm not going to lie and say I'm not thrilled that we're the top-ranked team in the Pacific Northwest. But I also love helping the kids see what they can do when they're willing to give themselves a chance and put the effort in. You taught me that, Morgan."

"I did?" The two words came out a little breathless.

His eyes were dark and steady on hers. "You did."

Morgan had been expecting this conversation to be difficult, given everything that had happened between them, but it didn't feel hard at all. No, the only difficult thing about it was how incredibly good it was to be close to him again. And they *were* close, sitting just inches away from one another with his arm brushing against hers as he told her about the summer football camps where they took in students from off the island. Another coach might have talked only about plays or wins, but Brian's passion was all about how much he was able to do for his students.

"I'm really glad you're going to replant the old Walker plot," he said. "It's been empty for too long."

"It's probably a bit of a mess by now, but it should be a good test bed to work on ingredients. I don't know if I'll really be able to find ingredients here that I couldn't find somewhere else, but it still felt really important to me to come back to the island to at least try."

He nodded. "It isn't just about what you're growing or how you're using it for the makeup line, is it? It's about your roots, too."

Yet again, he understood so much, understood all of the things that she hadn't even known how to put into words herself.

She was still reeling from that realization when he said in a quiet but sure voice, "I never stopped thinking about you, Morgan. I know the timing wasn't right when we were kids, that you could have never stayed and I could have never gone. Things were too complicated back then, regardless of what we felt or how much we loved each other. But we could try again now. We're both in a much better place to make it work this time, because we aren't kids anymore."

They certainly weren't, but did that actually make things any easier? If anything, it just meant that by now they both had their lives set up *exactly* the way they wanted, in the places they wanted. Places that were three thousand miles apart.

Of course, there was a part of her that wished life could be so simple that they could snap their fingers and have everything they wanted without ever having to make difficult choices. Especially when just being in the same room as Brian made her feel more alive than she had since she was eighteen years old and he'd kissed her for the very last time.

But she couldn't just turn her back on the life she'd created, could she? Not when it was finally turning into everything she'd ever dreamed of. Nor could she ask him to leave the island behind when it was obvious that he not only belonged here, but that he was *needed* here by his students, the football team and the community that depended on him to be a strong leader for their kids.

"Brian, it's good seeing you. Amazing, actually," she admitted. "But I'm not back on the island for good. I'm back here for only a few weeks to get the garden set up for my makeup line. Once it's planted and I find a balance of ingredients that works, I'll be heading back to New York. I just can't be here longer than part of the summer. Not when the network is giving me my own makeover show and I'll need to be back in the city to shoot it in their studios. This whole trip to the island, the makeup line, everything...it's really just tying in with that."

Brian didn't try to argue with anything she said, but Morgan knew better than to think that he was giving in. What did it say that she still knew every nuance of Brian's expressions, especially the determined one?

"I know that you've got the life you always dreamed of," he finally said. "But I also know that last time I let you go without a fight, and I've regretted it ever since."

A crazy part of her wanted to say, *I did, too.* But she made the rational part speak up instead. "You know why I left."

"You felt like you had to leave everything here—your family, the island, me—to become who you wanted to be. I understood where you were coming from, Morgan. That it was never easy to live under a microscope on the island because you were a Walker, and that you chafed at the smallness, the quiet, even the sureness of knowing you would always be taken care of by the people who loved you. I didn't want to be the one who was going to stand in the way of your success, didn't want you to resent me, so I didn't fight. But I was wrong. So damned wrong. And now that you know who you are and what you're capable of—and I know those same things about myself—the fact is that I still want what I've always wanted. *You.* So this time, I'm not going to just stand back while you walk away. I thought love meant needing to let you go, but now I think it's just the opposite. Love means giving everything I am to fight for you to stay."

"I think"—Morgan pushed away from the table and stood up—"we'd better head back to the cars."

On the walk to the bar, things had felt surprisingly comfortable, and she'd almost been able to believe that they could "just be friends." Now, however, she knew how wrong that was. Because when he'd made his impassioned speech, every cell in her body had wanted to say, *Yes, I'll stay,* right then and there.

They were almost back to her car when Brian reached for her hand. She was so stunned by the sweet feel of his warm skin against hers that she didn't even think to pull away.

A moment later, he was pulling her into his arms. Warm, strong arms that had always been her favorite place in the world. Another man might have tried to kiss her to prove his point that they were still meant to be together, but Brian's hug was almost more powerful than any kiss would have been.

His hug was not only a reminder of old times and their unstoppable attraction...it was also, clearly, a promise. A promise that he wasn't going to make things easy on her this time.

Because he was going to fight for her to stay.

"It really is good to have you back, Morgan. I'll see you tomorrow."

CHAPTER FIVE

Morgan felt dizzy and breathless as she drove the convertible to her family's house, barely able to concentrate enough to make the short journey safely in the unfamiliar car. She couldn't stop thinking about how good it had felt to finally be back in his arms.

She pulled up to the big, sprawling home she'd grown up in with her four sisters and saw Michael Bennet hammering something on the porch. Any other hot-blooded woman would see a tall, dark-haired, muscular guy like him and take a second look, but he'd always been like a brother to her after moving in with her family when his parents passed away when he was a teenager.

"Welcome home, Morgan." Michael gave her a warm hug. "I'll get your bags." He let out a low whistle when he saw her car. "Nice ride."

"My assistant who took care of booking the

rental doesn't quite get what the island is like," she tried to explain.

Michael lifted out the first couple of cases, his muscles straining through the cotton of his T-shirt as he did so. "How much stuff did you *bring*?" He stopped and studied her more carefully. "Are you moving back to the island for good?"

"No, I'm just here for a few weeks this summer," Morgan assured him. And herself. Because even though Brian was more tempting than any man had been—or ever would be—she couldn't possibly stay on Walker Island. "I've got too many things going on in New York to stay longer than that." She grabbed the final bag out of the trunk, then said, "I can't wait to see everyone."

Emily was stirring a big pot of spaghetti Bolognese as Morgan walked in. Her sister left it simmering, hurrying over to hug her. Frequent hugs were one of the loveliest things about coming back home, especially when people in the city usually barely made eye contact.

It always amazed Morgan how people could say that all the Walker sisters looked alike, never looking beyond their blond hair and blue eyes. Emily, in particular, had always stood apart to Morgan. She was taller, for one thing, and was certainly beautiful, but she had always been a little more serious, a little more grounded. Paige had her lithe dancer's figure that she always toned down with sweatpants and workout clothes. Rachel had that ultra practical "I'm a mom" way of dressing so that nothing could get ruined if little Charlotte happened to get paint or something worse on them. And, of course, their youngest sister, Hanna, had fun streaks of color in her hair and an unparalleled zest for life. Though it had been a month since the wedding, Morgan was still a little stunned that Hanna had been the first of her sisters to get married. Especially to a Peterson. But, oh, it was just *lovely* to see how happy Hanna and Joel were.

Grams, who had been sitting at the kitchen table tapping away on a laptop with a two-fingered determination that was surprisingly speedy, also got up to give Morgan a warm hug. There was nothing quite as comforting as sinking into her grandmother's arms. No place quite as safe.

"It's good to have you back," Emily said once Grams went back to her computer, "though I thought you'd get in earlier.

"I headed straight over to the school to meet with my new interns."

Emily gave her a look that made it clear she knew Morgan wasn't mentioning one other *very* important person she'd met with. Still, all she said for the time being was, "Rachel is going to be over soon with Charlotte. Paige called to say that she's going to have to work late at the studio, but will come find you tomorrow to catch up."

Even as kids, Paige had barely set foot out of the dance studio when she didn't have to. Morgan was only a year younger than Paige, and while the two of them were really close, some days it felt like they couldn't be more different. If Paige had the opportunity to be on TV, especially off the island—and there was no question that she was good enough to dance in major productions—she'd probably run the other way. Dancing on the island always seemed to be enough for her.

When Emily went back to her cooking, Morgan moved to sit beside Ava at the big table. Her grandmother was still incredibly beautiful in her seventies, with the elegant poise of a dancer, her blue eyes as deep and sharp as they had ever been.

"I didn't know you had a laptop, Grams."

"It's all this fan mail I've been getting since your sister's documentary came out. It's great fun, but it can take some doing keeping up with it all."

Morgan smiled at that. Hanna's documentary about the Peterson-Walker feud had made quite a splash, and Morgan was thrilled about it. That is, as long as her grandmother's newfound fame wasn't too much for Grams to deal with. Fame could be fun, but there were also downsides to losing privacy and feeling as if you were living under a magnifying glass.

Michael came into the kitchen. "Morgan, I've taken those bags up to your old room. And, Emily, the porch step is as good as new now."

"Thanks, although you know you didn't need to take time away from your crew to work on it. I would have gotten around to it eventually," Emily insisted.

"Yes, but now you don't have to."

"I think it was very kind of you to help, Michael," Ava said, shooting Emily a pointed look.

Emily and Michael had been this way with each other for as long as Morgan could remember. When, she wondered, would they both finally wake up and see what had been right there in front of them since they were kids? Because she had no doubt whatsoever that they were meant to be.

"I hope you'll be staying for dinner, Michael?"

"Only if there's enough," he said.

Emily rolled her eyes and told him, "When is there ever *not* enough food in this house?"

He grinned at Morgan. "Looks like I'm staying, then." But as soon as he sat down on the other side of Ava to help her with a new program she had installed on her computer, Emily took Morgan's arm and pulled her into the hallway.

"So, how was seeing Brian again?"

"I..." How could she put something into words that she hadn't yet figured out? "I was surprised to learn that he's my interns' science teacher." She hoped her sister hadn't noticed that Morgan hadn't actually answered her question.

"All the kids love him," Emily said. "He's a great teacher, and you know how interested he always was in science." But since she could clearly see that Morgan had been thrown off by seeing Brian again, she added in a gentler voice, "He volunteered for the position, and as both the science teacher and football coach, he really was the perfect choice to oversee those two students. I thought about overseeing them myself, but it really has to be about what's best for Natalie and Tad."

"You're right," Morgan said, "it does." She wanted her two interns to get as much as possible from working with her on the garden. One of the main reasons she'd decided to hire high school students was that she wanted to give kids from the island a chance to improve their prospects out in the rest of the world. It was a great opportunity for both Natalie and Tad, and an escape route if they didn't want to end up stuck on the island.

Even so...

"You should have told me that Brian would be involved, Emily. I was so shocked when he walked up with them that I'm pretty sure I made a huge fool of myself."

Emily hugged her again. "I'm sorry. I was just so afraid that if you knew he was involved you might not come home at all. I know how complicated things were for you with Brian and how hard you've worked not to hear anything about him all these years. I was kind of hoping that this way it would be like a Band-Aid. You know, you close your eyes, rip it off, and find out that it didn't hurt so much after all." But she looked really concerned as she added, "Did everything go okay with him? Because if you're too upset about it, I can see if I can find a replacement."

Morgan thought back to everything Brian had said about not fighting for her after high school graduation and always regretting it. She thought, yet again, about his arms around her. And then she thought about how much she was looking forward to seeing him again tomorrow.

No doubt about it, she should take Emily up on her offer to pull Brian from the project, because it was the safest way to make sure they didn't get entangled in each other's lives again. But the thought of seeing Brian again only in passing sent such a sharp pang into the center of Morgan's chest, that in the end, she simply gave her sister a reassuring smile and said, "You don't need to find a replacement, Emily. Everything went fine."

CHAPTER SIX

Morgan drove over to the garden early the next morning. It was a little way from the houses and stores on the island, up toward the large berry growing fields that Morgan's Great-Grandfather William Walker had planted all those years ago, back before her grandfather had sold them off to fund the school.

Morgan, of all people, couldn't blame William Walker II for wanting to follow his dreams, but she was glad that he had thought to hold back this one acre, at least. She used to come here often as a child to pick berries from the few old remaining bushes and plant her own little patches of flowers, and her mother had shown her how to push seeds down into the soil and water them with a tiny watering can while her father looked on. After her mother's death, Morgan had continued to keep up the flowers, feeling sometimes as if the large blue blooms on the Great Blue Lobelia bushes were her mother's way of sprinkling magic onto them from above.

But now that she hadn't been back for more than a few days at a time over the past seven years, berry seeds from the nearby fields had drifted in, making for a mess of brambles and tangles, nettles and weeds. It was going to take a lot of work to turn it back into the bountiful vegetable, fruit and flower garden it had once been. Yet she only felt *more* determined to make it work, and not just for her organic makeup line. Morgan wanted to feel as if her mother was still looking down on her, wanted to pretend that they were out working side by side with the land and the water all around them.

The ringtone on her phone jolted her out of her memories. "The contracts are looking exactly the way we wanted them to," Juliet said as soon as Morgan picked up. "The distributers are on board, and the production company for the series is looking happy with the format. They want to talk to you about set designs sometime soon and work out a shooting schedule. I also wanted to remind you to take lots of pictures and get them up on your social media pages. It's time to start building the online buzz about the series so that we're ready when the pilot program goes out."

"I'll get them up soon," Morgan promised, then checked to make sure there wasn't anything urgent that needed her attention before she hung up.

The network's marketing team had loved the angle of Morgan bringing her family's garden back to life to produce ingredients for her makeup line. With luck, by the time her line and the show came out together, people would already be so caught up in the photos and videos that she planned to post over the next several weeks that they would automatically be hooked when the show began to air and her makeup line finally hit stores.

But as she breathed in the soft scents of the berry fields around her, Morgan knew this garden could never just be boiled down to a PR angle. Not when it was a *huge* part of who she was, even if she was the only member of the current generation of Walkers who had inherited the family's green thumb.

Morgan used her phone to take a few pictures of the wild, overgrown acre, working to make sure that she got the light right and framed the plants so that they drew the eye into the picture.

By the time she'd taken and uploaded her final picture for the time being, Brian's classic Mustang pulled up to the edge of the field. It looked so incongruous sitting next to her convertible. And so much more fitting for the island.

Tad was the first out of Brian's car. Morgan tried not to laugh as the big football player practically sprinted around to Natalie's side to open her door for her. But she couldn't hold that laugh in when Natalie beat him to it, getting out on her own, completely oblivious to Tad's attempt at chivalry.

"Young love," Morgan said softly to herself as she saw the crestfallen look on her male intern's face. He really did have it bad for the girl, didn't he?

For her part, Natalie was too busy rushing over to Morgan to pay any attention to Tad. The teenager was dressed in jeans and boots that looked like they were designed for slogging through the mud, yet she'd still brought her folder with her. From the speed with which she covered the ground to Morgan, she was obviously eager to begin.

"What are we doing first?" Natalie asked. But before Morgan could answer, she said, "I have some ideas, if you want to see them."

"I would love to see them." Morgan definitely didn't want to discourage that kind of enthusiasm.

Natalie handed over a half-dozen sheets of paper, each with a possible design for the plot sketched out in multicolored pens. Everything was carefully labeled and measured. Clearly, Natalie had come up here more than once on her own time.

"These are really impressive," Morgan said. She wasn't just being polite, either. The sketches *were* impressive. Natalie already understood which berry varieties could be mixed in with herbs and the spots where particular varieties had to be given their own room. There were also paths built into the design to allow for people to easily work on the plants and beds. "You've obviously put in a lot of work on these."

"Mr. Russell helped me with them," Natalie admitted. "He knew all about the way the garden used to be laid out and what grew really well."

Of course he would have. Brian had been here so many times with Morgan when they were kids that he knew this acre of land almost as well as she did.

"It still sounds like you put in a lot of work, Natalie. Thank you. I'm really, really impressed."

Just then, Brian walked over, carrying a beautiful bouquet of flowers. One that was almost identical to the displays that had decorated their prom, wild flowers from this garden and a couple of other nearby fields that combined into a riot of color.

"Good morning."

He put the bouquet in her hands, and she was breathing in the sweet and spicy scents even as she said, "Thank you, Brian. You...you shouldn't have."

He stared at her for a long moment, his dark eyes intense and full of longing that he obviously wasn't going to try to hide from her. "I wanted to. I hope you like them."

"I do." How could she not? "I love the flowers,

thank you."

Which was why she needed to take several steps back and turn away from him to put the flowers in a safe place, to give herself a little time to recover. Even as she did so, however, something told her she could take all the time in the world and she still wouldn't be able to shake the sweet, warm feeling that being with Brian gave her.

Realizing Tad and Natalie were waiting for her to direct them, she moved back toward the group and held up Natalie's plans in her hand, comparing them to the weed-choked garden plot. The difference between the end goal and their starting point was almost too much to comprehend, but they could do it if they tried. Morgan was sure of it.

"Let's go with this plan," she said, pointing to the top design. "It's going to take a lot of work, but it's the best design for the space."

"There's nothing wrong with putting in some hard work to get what you want," Brian said. He handed out thick gloves and shears to the two kids. "We've got a lot of brambles to clear."

"We could start over that way," Tad suggested, pointing to the upper left corner of the plot. "If we get a lot of the larger stuff out, then it will be easier to get in to work on the rest."

As Brian encouraged the teenagers to work out their action plan for the morning, Morgan could see what a great teacher he was, very patient and encouraging. Here was yet another reason it was going to be *so* hard not to fall for him again, especially while working this close to one another day in and day out for several weeks...

Working to push that thought aside, Morgan pulled on her own gardening gloves and got to work. Honestly, it was good being outside, doing something physical in the sun, rather than being in a studio for hours to film what would end up being just a few minutes after editing.

After a while, Morgan moved to work with Tad on a section that needed two people to dig away at it. She appreciated that he wasn't at all afraid of working hard.

"Ms. Walker?"

"Why don't you call me Morgan?" she said with a smile.

"Okay, um, Morgan...you know how you liked the flowers Coach Russell brought you? Do all girls like getting flowers?"

Morgan couldn't hold back her smile. She suspected that if Tad had a defensive line charging toward him, he wouldn't flinch, but just the thought of trying to find a way to woo Natalie obviously had him tied in knots.

"It depends on the girl, but if I had to guess, I'd say that most do."

Under any other circumstances, Morgan might have given Tad a little advice about actually asking Natalie out. Yet for as much as Tad obviously liked Natalie, Morgan simply couldn't see how things could work out for the two of them in the long run. Not when Tad was an island boy through and through, and Natalie was clearly going to have a big future ahead of her off the island. Probably a long way off.

No, Morgan told herself as she yanked at a weed with all her might, it was better that Natalie and Tad remained just friends. That way, neither of them would have to know how bad it hurt when it came time to say good-bye.

CHAPTER SEVEN

Brian had never much enjoyed pulling weeds, but today digging deep into the worst of the tangles was the perfect way to work out his frustrations.

Lord knew there were plenty of frustrations for him to choose from right then. How did Morgan always manage to look so incredibly beautiful, even while cutting through brambles? How was he going to be able to keep from staring at her for too long and wanting her so much that he could actually feel the ache in the center of his chest from it? And how could he have ever been so stupid as to let her leave without a fight all those years ago?

Every instinct told him he should go over to Morgan and kiss her. Just take her in his arms and make her his again. Especially when he *knew* that she was still attracted to him from the way her skin flushed and her breathing sped up whenever he was near. Their physical connection was obvious. It had *always* been obvious. What they felt for one another had never been in doubt, so why not take that to its logical conclusion? Why not take back what they'd once had?

But he knew why, knew all the reasons he couldn't just grab her in the middle of the garden and kiss her. He couldn't risk scaring her off. Not when he had blown his chance with her once before by letting her walk away and didn't want to blow it again now by moving too fast. The hug he'd given her the night before, along with today's bouquet of flowers, were enough of a starting point. Small gestures, but ones that showed Morgan he was serious about wanting to make things work this time.

"What do you think we should work on next, Mr. Russell?" Natalie asked.

Grateful for the break from the questions that kept circling over and over inside his head, Brian looked over what Natalie had done so far. "Why don't you tell me what you think needs our attention?"

"We could probably do a little more clearing of these heavier vines between the bushes, but I think it will be good if we leave the blueberries and the raspberries in together since the soil seems to be more acidic at this end of the plot."

"That's a good analysis, Natalie. You're really enjoying this project already, aren't you?"

"Oh yes! Getting to work with Ms. Walker like this is such an amazing opportunity."

"It really is, isn't it?" Just getting to be near Morgan had always been amazing for him. So amazing that even seven years hadn't been enough time for the hole in his heart to close.

"Plus, with all of these different species of plants in such a small environment, it's so interesting to see all the ways they work together—which ones tangle and choke one another and which ones give each other the chance to grow. And then after we harvest the plants, we're going to get to explore the science of getting exactly the right chemistry for the makeup."

Working together and *chemistry.* So much of life came down to both of those things. Especially his relationship with Morgan.

Brian shook his head and turned his focus back to the heavy brambles in the center of the plot. Getting them out by hand was hard work, but it was the only way they could proceed without damaging the plants they actually wanted to keep growing. Besides, he had no objections to the job taking a little longer if it meant that he could spend more time around Morgan.

Just then, he saw Tad slowly making his way over to Natalie and smiled as he realized he wasn't the only one happy just to get to be near a girl he couldn't stop thinking about. Only, as

Natalie never lifted her head from the job, Tad looked more despondent by the second.

"Hey, Tad," Brian called out, "come over and give me a hand with these, would you?"

"Sure, Coach." They worked to lift several heavy wooden posts out of the way before tad said, "Can I ask you a question?"

"Sure. What's on your mind?"

"You know how you gave Ms. Walker flowers? Was that your way of asking her out?"

Brian wasn't sure how to explain his relationship with Morgan to one of his students, or even if he should. "I've known her for a really long time, but it's been awhile since we've seen each other, so things are kind of complicated between us. That's why I figured flowers might be a nice way to try to break the ice."

"Yeah," Tad said with another glance across to Natalie. "I can see how things can get really complicated really fast, even if you see each other every day."

Brian had seen the way Tad had looked at Natalie ever since she had set off some small, multicolored fireworks she'd made in class a few months back. All the other kids had been staring at the display, but Tad had only had eyes for her.

"Come on, Tad," Brian said, "we both still have a lot of work to do."

He let the teenager get back to work pulling up brambles near Natalie, who glanced up briefly when he came near and gave him a big smile.

Brian headed in the opposite direction toward Morgan, and when she looked up and also smiled, he thought he caught a flash of pleasure—and heat—in her eyes.

Who would have thought that he would find himself stuck in the same situation as one of the teenagers he taught, trying to make headway with a beautiful woman? At the moment, it seemed that getting through an opposing football team's defenses would have certainly been a lot easier than the task either of them faced.

CHAPTER EIGHT

"Are you already napping? It's not even lunchtime!"

Morgan's eyes snapped open as she shot off the couch. She'd just been having the nicest dream where Brian was...no, better not to think about that.

"I'm awake," she said sleepily.

"Sure you are," Rachel retorted. "Just the way Charlotte claims to be awake before she snuggles back down under her covers and tries to pretend that I'm not there."

"I'm jet-lagged," Morgan said with a groan, but when she saw there was no point trying to pretend she wasn't still completely addicted to naps the way she'd been as a young girl, she asked, "Where's my favorite niece? "

"Charlotte's at the dance studio with Paige and Grams while Michael is downstairs helping install some new software on my computer," Rachel said. "They're doing a butterfly dance workshop at the studio. Charlotte loves butterflies so much that we stenciled her bedroom walls with butterflies in every possible color."

"I wish you had told me about it," Morgan said. "I would have painted her face to look like a butterfly before she left for the studio today."

"She would have loved that," Rachel agreed with a smile.

Morgan got the feeling that her sister didn't do as much of that these days as she should have. Rachel had been the carefree, wild one when they were kids. But now that she had a daughter and worked for one of the local insurers, she was so careful all the time...

Morgan got up and followed her sister into the kitchen, where Michael was sitting at the kitchen table with a laptop in front of him. "Hey, sleepyhead."

She yawned and waved before opening the fridge to see what there was to drink. She hadn't heard him come in, which meant he'd obviously been there for a little while. Clearly, she'd napped longer than she'd intended.

"You're here *again*?" Emily said to Michael as she also walked into the kitchen. "Don't you ever feel like seeing the inside of your own place?"

"But then I wouldn't get this kind of warm welcome," Michael teased, making Emily smile despite herself.

Michael had always been like a brother to them growing up, and all the sisters, except the one who wouldn't admit that she was head over heels in love with him, were perfectly happy with him wandering around as he pleased. Plus, he always did so much around the house, from fixing the porch to repairing the roof and the pipes in the kitchen.

Why was Emily so determined to ignore the spark that existed between them, even though everyone else could see it? And why did Rachel have to fall in love with a guy who had seemed great until he got her pregnant and left her to raise their baby completely alone? If only, Morgan wished, everyone could get exactly what they wanted from their lives.

Which left one obvious question. What did *she* want?

"I know that look," Rachel said. "It's the same look you always had when you were worried about an assignment when we were kids. Do I need to get out the hot chocolate?"

After their mother's death, Emily had done a lot to look after the rest of them, but as the second-oldest, Rachel had been there, too, always ready with unconditional sympathy. In a lot of ways, she'd been the strong one. It was strange how things had changed. There was something almost fragile about her sister now.

"Since none of us are ten anymore," Morgan

said, "how about we make it wine?"

Emily had already grabbed a bottle and three glasses. "You have until we finish the bottle to tell us what's going on."

Morgan knew better than to try to argue. With two of her sisters ganging up on her because they loved her, she had no chance of getting away with her secrets intact. In any case, she wasn't sure she wanted to hold it inside anymore. Not when she needed to talk to someone about everything that had happened since she'd gotten back on the island yesterday. Needed them to tell her that she wasn't crazy and that she was doing the right thing by keeping her distance from Brian.

Leaving Michael in the kitchen to work on the computer, the three sisters settled down on the couch in the living room, each with a glass of berry wine that had come from the other side of the island. Emily generally didn't see the point in buying things from off the island when she believed everything they needed was already there. In this case, she had a point, since it was really fantastic wine.

"So," Emily said, "what happened with Brian today out at the garden?"

"It's not just Brian," Morgan insisted. But when her sisters gave her *that* look, she admitted, "Okay, maybe it mostly is about him, but there's also this thing with the interns that I don't know how to deal with."

"There's a problem with the interns?" Emily asked. "I thought they would be just right for your project. I mean, they're both good kids, so if they're doing something wrong, especially so early on, then you should talk to them. They probably just need a little extra guidance."

"No, they're doing a great job with the land. In fact, you should see the plans Natalie drew up. They're incredible. And Tad will work until he drops, which is super helpful considering how much thick brush there was for all of us to clear away. It's just that Tad is obviously head over heels for Natalie, and while I know that Natalie has her own big dreams off the island—"

"Don't get involved," Emily said firmly.

"Wait a minute," Rachel said. "We don't even know what Morgan was about to say."

"Trust me," Emily continued, "you don't get involved in the love lives of students. Ever. They won't end up thanking you for interfering, not when both of their hearts end up broken and they're filled with angst."

Rachel thought about it for a few seconds before finally agreeing. "Emily's probably right. Besides, I'm pretty sure you're only bringing those kids up to try to distract us from the important stuff. Namely, what's up with you and Brian?"

Morgan was on the verge of telling her sisters that there was no *me and Brian*, but that would have been a lie. And she just couldn't lie to them.

"He wants us to get back together." Both of her sisters' eyebrows flew up as she added, "He gave me flowers this morning, the same ones he gave me back in high school at our prom. And yesterday when we went for a drink together—"

"Hold on," Rachel said. "You went for a drink with him?"

"Just to catch up. It shouldn't have meant anything. It wasn't *supposed* to mean anything. But he ended up saying that while he understands why I had to leave seven years ago, now that I'm back and we're both adults instead of kids, he wants us to try again."

"Wow, that's—"

"But I'm *not* back," Morgan continued, cutting Emily off. "At least, not for long. He was saying how he's going to fight for me this time and how he's never stopped regretting letting me go because he's still in love with me, but that's just *nuts*, right? I mean, if he left this island he would be miserable, and I'm all settled in New York."

Emily refilled all of their glasses then said, "You're the only one who can decide what you need to do, Morgan. You need to think about what there is for you there and what there is for you here."

"It's obviously a shock, Brian just coming out with all of his feelings like that," Rachel added, "but at least now you know what's in his heart. The question is, what are you feeling...and what's in your heart for him?"

"When I saw him again yesterday, I tried to ignore the sparks that immediately shot off between us, but when he hugged me, I never wanted to leave his arms. Which is crazy, because we all know it would never work. Yes, we're adults now, but, if anything, that only means we're more set in stone with our careers and lives on opposite coasts."

She could tell Emily wanted to say something more, but just then Morgan's phone dinged with an email from Juliet saying the studio wanted to lock her into a single location for the shooting of her show. Thinking about how Brian had said his favorite segment had been when she'd gone on the road—and how she'd felt exactly the same way—Morgan stood up and said, "Sorry, I need to deal with something my assistant just alerted me to."

* * *

After Morgan left the room, Michael walked in and said, "Don't do it," to Rachel and Emily.

"Do what?" Emily asked, but it was clear from the flush in her cheeks that she knew exactly what he was talking about.

"Interfere with Morgan and Brian. Or am I wrong and that's not what both of you are thinking of doing?"

Rachel cracked first. "I was just thinking that it might be nice if...well...what if..."

"What if we could get Morgan to stay?" Emily

finished for her.

"I know how much you both love her and why you want her to stay. I do, too." Even more than they wanted her to stay on the island, though, he knew that they wanted their sister to find love again. Still, that didn't change his advice. "But even if you think you'd be helping her, and him, too, by meddling, we all know that if they're going to work things out—or not—they need to do it all by themselves."

CHAPTER NINE

The garden behind the historical society wasn't large, certainly not as large as the Walker plot, but it had always been one of Morgan's favorite places. Though it had been planted only twenty years before, it seemed much older, squeezing a grand old mansion's flower garden into a space half the size. She'd come to the patio that overlooked the flowers and small trees as a kid to get her schoolwork done whenever it didn't seem likely to happen in a house full of sisters, and now she worked there again, going through her email.

So far she'd composed a reply to the network about why she thought it would be far better if they filmed her makeover show on the road versus bringing her subjects into the New York studio every time. She'd also read through Juliet's research on potential supply chains and had sent a couple of messages to celebrities she'd worked with to feel out the likelihood of them coming on her show.

"I thought I'd find you here," Brian said.

She looked up with surprise—and pleasure she couldn't even begin to suppress—as he came up onto the porch to sit down next to her. He'd cleaned up after working in the garden that morning, but there was still a wonderfully earthy, outdoors feel to him. She couldn't imagine certain people working in an office, and Brian was definitely one of them.

"Some things don't change," Morgan agreed, putting away her laptop as she accepted that she wasn't going to get any work done with Brian here. Not when being this close to him completely scrambled her brain...and the rest of her, too. "Especially on Walker Island."

"Some things have definitely changed. Lots of things, actually."

Morgan should have just let it go, but she suddenly couldn't stop herself from challenging him. "Name three."

"I can do better than that." Brian stood up, holding out a hand to her. "Let me show you what's different. Unless of course..." He didn't finish, just let his challenge linger between them.

Morgan knew the last thing she needed to do right then was go on a field trip around the island with Brian. After everything he'd said, after he'd held her in his arms, and after the flowers he'd given her, saying yes to this would probably only give him the wrong idea. But how could she run from the challenge in his eyes? And how could she possibly pretend that she didn't love to spend time with him?

Besides, she *would* like to see the changes to the island. Morgan had been back a few times since she'd left, a day here and there for Grams' birthday or one of Charlotte's recitals, but it had always been a super quick visit. In and out, with no time to do more than toast a bride or carve a Thanksgiving turkey.

"Okay," Morgan said as she stood up. "Although the way I remember things growing up, the boats in the harbor getting a fresh coat of paint was a big deal."

Brian laughed as he drew her to her feet, and for a moment they were close enough that she could smell the wonderfully clean, masculine scent of him.

He slung her heavy bag over his shoulder, then led the way out of the historical society into town. He gestured to the left, where a small boutique now sat. "Do you remember what used to be there?"

"The old candy store." Morgan could remember saving up her money to buy plenty of sweet stuff as a kid, although she had to admit that these days, the current contents of the windows were probably more to her taste.

"That's right," Brian said. "Mrs. Kiriakis sold

her store about a year after you left."

He led the way down a winding lane where Morgan couldn't remember anything much being there when she'd left. Just a few old, empty workshops. Today, though, they were open to the outside world as studios for working artists. What had been a dull, ordinary spot had sprung to life with a sculptor working on a bust, a couple of painters discussing a half-finished canvas, and a sketch artist doing quick but excellent drawings of passersby.

"Do you mind if I draw the two of you?" the man asked as they came closer. "It will only take a few minutes." Agreeing that they could spare the time, she and Brian stood together, hand in hand, while the artist sketched with charcoal and pastels, looking them over with a critical eye.

"You really do look good together," he said when he was done and showed them the picture. He'd caught their connection so perfectly, and Morgan was more pleased than she wanted to admit when he gave them the drawing.

"Come on," Brian said after she very carefully tucked the beautiful drawing in between two folders in her bag so that it wouldn't wrinkle or smear. "There are a couple more places I'd like to show you."

He took her up in the direction of an old lookout point where they'd once gone on a date, just enjoying being with one another as they'd stared out over the ocean. A small building had been built on the site with a sign beside it that said *Walker Island Ornithological Station*.

"Bird watchers have taken our spot?"

She didn't realize what she'd said—*our spot*—until she saw the warmth, and the yearning, in Brian's eyes. But he didn't draw out the moment, just simply said, "Come inside."

The interior of the small building was similar to the whale-watching stations around the island where the marine biologists congregated. However, where those had pictures of whales mixed in with sonar equipment, this one was filled with pictures of coastal birds, along with plenty of telescopes. A middle-aged man and woman were staring out over the island and down toward the sea through two side-by-side telescopes.

"I'm telling you, Harold, I know an osprey when I see one. I do have a PhD in ornithology, you know."

"So do I, and there aren't any that make their home on the island, Lisa."

"Until now."

Brian cleared his throat, and they both looked up with smiles. "Hello, Brian," the woman said.

"Hi, Lisa. I hope you don't mind me coming round like this. Harold, Lisa, I'd like you to meet Morgan Walker. Morgan, this is Dr. Bernstein and Dr. Bernstein."

"You're married?" Morgan asked.

"Was it the arguing that gave it away?" Lisa joked right before Harold looked at her with his heart in his eyes.

"Yes, we are, and I'm the luckiest man in the world."

Brian was grinning as he said, "Harold and Lisa have been running a research project looking into the island's birds for the last couple of years."

A couple of years? It was weird thinking that this building had been sitting on one of Morgan's favorite spots on the island for a couple of years, and she hadn't known about it.

"I thought most of the research teams from the universities came here for the whales?"

"Certainly that's the main focus of research on the island," Harold agreed. "But there are whole new avenues of research when it comes to a microclimate like the one on the island. Species can be introduced and change things around them very quickly."

"Like ospreys," Lisa said with a little smirk on her pretty face.

"That was *not* an osprey."

Brian nodded to the door as the couple continued their argument from where they'd been interrupted, and Morgan took the hint.

"I encourage students to come up here to get a taste of research," Brian said. "And they usually come away with a lot of new knowledge...at least when those two aren't sparring."

"Don't they scare off the birds?" Morgan

teased.

"You'd think so, wouldn't you? But you can see how much they love each other, underneath it all. And the bird observatory has been a really good addition to the island." He brushed a lock of hair away from her eyes before saying, "There's one more thing I want to show you."

Morgan nodded, although actually it felt a little strange to see these changes in the one place that she'd always believed would never change.

Brian led the way back down the hill to the old oak tree at the heart of town, and she looked around, wondering what could possibly be different here. "This all looks the same. What did you want to show me that's so different?"

Brian drew her over to the tree. There in the bark was a heart, not carved with any initials, but simply with the words *You and Me*. It had been the lyrics of the song playing back at their prom when he'd pulled her into his arms and kissed her with all the love in his heart.

"Some things are supposed to change," Brian told her, his voice as serious as she'd ever heard it. "But some things never, ever will."

CHAPTER TEN

The next morning, Morgan drove out to the Walker plot, determined that this time she wasn't going to let herself get distracted or pulled into any other "adventures" with Brian. They would simply finish clearing and fertilizing the areas where they would be growing new plants. That was it. In fact, the moment they were done, Morgan was going to go home, lock herself inside and not come out.

Especially not for sentimental trips around town where she would spend half the time thinking that a gorgeous, off-limits man was about to kiss her, only to be disappointed when he didn't.

When Brian had shown her the tree with the love heart carved in it, Morgan had stood there, desperate for the feel of his lips on hers again...but all he'd done was bring her back home, leaving her at the door, not even coming inside to say hi to her family. Certainly not giving her the kind of good-bye kiss that he used to.

She should have been happy about that. Should have been glad that he wasn't forcing her into a situation where she'd have to push him away to make sure they didn't end up hurting each other again when she left. But she didn't feel happy or glad about it at all.

Why did everything have to be so complicated?

Pulling a few weeds might have helped to deal with the sheer frustration of being around Brian and not knowing *what* to feel, but they'd done a good job clearing nearly all of them away the previous day. Another thing that was obviously good but that she could have done without right then.

And when Brian finally did arrive, walking over to her with Natalie and Tad beside him, the way he said, "Hi, Morgan," sounded far too smug to her ears. Almost as if he knew just how badly he'd twisted her into knots by coming close...but not *nearly* close enough. Only Brian would have fought for her in such a sneaky, brilliant way, by making her want and need and desire him until she was nearly bursting with it!

"Hi, everyone," she said in as chipper and easy a voice as she could manage. It wouldn't do, not a bit, for Brian to think that she'd spent every single second since yesterday thinking about him. "Looks like we're ready to fertilize today."

"Mr. Russell had us study up on the science of fertilization," Natalie told her.

Tad nodded. "It's actually really cool how it all works."

Of course Brian had been able to turn the work her interns were doing into a really interesting science lesson. Darn him, why did he have to be so perfect? And gorgeous? And...

Enough already. She needed to keep her focus on the important job at hand, not on how much she wanted the one man she could never be with.

Morgan set off for the other side of the garden—as far as she could from Brian and all the temptation he presented—and when Natalie came with her, they poured the fertilizer onto areas that weren't already thick with useful plants, then raked it into the soil. With Natalie talking a mile a minute, Morgan was glad that she couldn't keep stewing over Brian and everything that had—and *hadn't*—happened yesterday. Although, Morgan noticed that Natalie occasionally paused in her monologue to look over to where Tad was working with an increasing flush growing on her cheeks.

Had Natalie finally started to notice Tad? Watching the two teenagers shoot each other looks when they each thought the other wasn't looking, Morgan was hit with a longing to go back to that time in high school when she and Brian had been so close. But even then, things hadn't been simple. Not when they had always been pulled between staying and going.

"Have you decided what the composition is going to be yet for your various pieces of the makeup line?" Natalie asked, breaking her out of her musings. "Because if you haven't settled on the exact ingredients, I was kind of hoping to help with the testing."

"You mean pulling weeds and raking in fertilizer all day wasn't all that you were hoping to get out of this internship?" Morgan teased. "I've done quite a bit of work already with some highly regarded scientists to work out the mineral components of my new line, but I'd love to involve you from this point forward in any way that I can. And once you have a better sense of where you'll be going to college next year, I'd be happy to talk with my colleagues near your campus to see if any of them have something interesting for you to work on."

"How can I ever thank you enough?"

Morgan grinned. "Keep raking."

The sun rose higher in the sky, the day turning out to be quite hot for the normally moderate island weather. It was hard work raking in the fertilizer, and Morgan barely found enough time to photograph the progress to tweet to her followers. She supposed some people probably thought she was crazy to do all this as preparation for her makeup line when she could have been sitting in a studio somewhere with a cool drink and assistants doing the heavy lifting.

But as she watched Brian working, his muscles moving strong and powerful beneath his shirt as he raked the soil, she had to admit that there were some compensations. Really *good* ones, even if they were only temporary.

Plus, it was so nice to be outside enjoying nature rather than hanging around on a set. Working in the garden, Morgan loved knowing that her efforts were not only going toward growing something beautiful but that she was also helping Tad and Natalie build up their transcripts, too.

It was lunchtime by the time they'd fertilized the whole plot. Which was very impressive, given that there were only four of them working on it. Yes, Morgan was hot and sweaty by the time it was done, but it was totally worth it.

Of course, Brian had come prepared with a large cooler of ice water and a couple of baskets full of picnic lunches. And Tad was clearly ready for lunch, because he descended on the first of the baskets like a whirlwind, shoveling a sandwich into his mouth before anyone else had a chance to even look through what was there.

"Tad," Brian suggested, "why don't you and Natalie take this lunch break to consider the best approach for the planting stage?"

"That's a great idea," Natalie immediately agreed, looking a little flushed for more reasons than just the heat.

Tad, of course, jumped at the opportunity to

go off with Natalie even quicker than he'd homed in on the picnic basket.

As soon as the two teenagers were gone, Brian pulled out a blanket and spread it on the ground in one of the shady spots on the plot. Despite vowing to leave for home as soon as they were done fertilizing, Morgan couldn't resist sitting down and helping herself to the picnic basket's contents. Especially when it turned out that Brian had packed her favorite spicy chicken wings.

"They look good together, don't they?" Brian said, nodding across to where Tad and Natalie were having their own picnic. Amazingly, Natalie had put down her pen and paper for the moment as she laughed at something Tad said.

"They do, but we both know that's not enough."

"Are you really telling me that you wouldn't be happy for them if they fell for each other?"

"She'll be leaving the island after graduation to follow her dreams. You know how clever she is."

"I do," Brian agreed, "but I don't see how all that automatically negates whatever they might end up feeling for one another."

Morgan looked at Tad and Natalie. They were both smiling, both happy, with that glow of first love that she remembered so well from high school. Morgan had often gone home after being with Brian feeling like she was floating.

"You know as well as I do that if anything does start with them, it can't last, because they're destined for two very different lives. A year from now when she's gone, they'll both be so busy with their new, exciting post-high-school lives that they probably won't even remember each other."

"You know that's not true," he said in a soft voice that resonated all the way through her. "I never forgot you, Morgan. Not for one second of the past seven years."

He didn't push her to say it back as they ate the rest of their picnic in silence, but he didn't need to. Not when they both knew that she hadn't forgotten him either.

And she was very much afraid that she never would.

CHAPTER ELEVEN

Doing makeup for one of Ava and Paige's dance studio shows was always so much fun for Morgan. Unlike a red carpet event, no one was shouting at anyone else, no one was storming around, and there was certainly no one phoning their agent to ask whether they were contractually obligated to wear a particular dress or brand of makeup.

It helped, of course, that Morgan had gotten a really good nap in before she headed down to the dance studio. Especially considering how sore she was from all the outdoor work she'd been doing on the garden plot. Sore was okay. Sore and exhausted wasn't. Not when she felt the bulk of her energy was spent trying to figure out how to stop noticing how sweet and gorgeous and sexy Brian was. At least for a few hours while she was here, she'd have a little breathing room to get her head back on straight.

"Do you know *all* the stars?" one of the girls she was making up asked her. "And do their makeup all the time?"

"I do know quite a few people in Hollywood, but I usually do their makeup only for big events and while they're filming."

"Are they all as pretty and thin as in the magazines?" another of the girls asked.

Morgan knew dangerous ground when she heard it. To most people, her business might be about making people look better, but for her it had always been more about showing people the sides of themselves that they kept hidden. It certainly wasn't about pushing girls to live up to the impossible.

"*No one* looks like that without the aid of photo enhancement," she assured the dancer. "Not even the biggest movie stars in the world."

"Really?" Both girls looked like they wanted to believe her but weren't sure they could.

"Yes, I promise you it's true. I've always loved to play up people's best features, but I wouldn't ever want to change who they really are."

"Is that what you're doing for us? Playing up our best features?"

"You're both absolutely beautiful," she told them, "so anything I do will be like the cherry on top of the sundae. Yummy, but not at all necessary."

She set to work on natural looks, and in a

short space of time, she had the girls staring at themselves with delight.

"I wish I could look like this all the time."

"I'll show you how. Like I said, I simply highlighted your natural beauty." Five minutes later, the girls thanked her profusely and another couple of dancers came to sit before her.

Morgan glanced over to where Paige was helping the girls warm up before the performance. When they were teenagers, Paige had played the black swan in *Swan Lake*, and Morgan had done her makeup. It was the only time Morgan could remember her talented sister agreeing to dance a major role, but apart from that one night, Paige had remained the only one of her sisters that Morgan hadn't been able to give a makeover.

One day, she vowed, she was going to get her hands on her sister, and then Paige wouldn't be able to hide her natural star quality any longer. But for today, Morgan had to keep her focus on reining in the kind of chaos that could only happen just before a performance. There were the girls warming up, the ones Morgan was just finishing making up, and several just starting to get into their costumes.

And, she realized as she heard a familiar low voice, Brian was now there, too.

Her breath went and her heart immediately started beating harder as she saw how incredibly handsome he was in his suit and open-collared shirt.

"Mr. Russell, you came!" The four girls she'd just finished making up clustered around him, obviously thrilled that he had shown up.

"I can't wait to see your show. I've heard great things about it from Ava and Paige. Thank you for inviting me."

They each told him about their specific roles, and after the girls walked away, Morgan said, "It's really sweet of you to come to support your students."

"I figure that if I go to all the football games, I should come to the dance recitals, too. It's a big deal to them," Brian said. "Their chance to be in the spotlight. I want to encourage them." Just the way he'd always encouraged her. "You've done a great job with their makeup, Morgan. They look beautiful, but still their own age."

Funny how after years of compliments from big stars and powerful people at TV networks, a few kind words from Brian felt so amazingly good. "I know just how hard the teenage years can be, so I wanted to show them how beautiful they already are so that they can really learn to love themselves."

"Love." His eyes were dark, intense, as he looked into hers. "That's what it all comes down to, isn't it?"

Before she could even attempt to think of a response, Paige rushed over. "Hi, Brian, glad you could make it. We're having a bit of an emergency with one of the props and could really use your help." She turned to Morgan and added, "We're also having trouble getting everyone into their costumes backstage. Help!"

* * *

By the time Morgan and Brian both made it into the audience to take their seats, only two remained in the very back corner. Ava and Paige always did a great job with their dance classes and the show really was good. Still, it was nearly impossible for Brian to keep his attention on the stage when Morgan was sitting so close beside him.

She was shifting in her seat as if she were trying to stretch her muscles, and guessing she had to be sore from the intense gardening work they'd done the past two days, he didn't think before reaching out to massage the muscles of her back. So many times in their past when they'd had long study sessions together hunched over their books, Morgan's muscles had cramped with tension. All these years later, he still remembered where to find all her tender spots.

"You haven't been stretching, have you?" he whispered, low enough that the music from the stage covered it. "Can I help?"

He was surprised—and totally thrilled—when she nodded and leaned into him. As he worked his fingers into her tight muscles, he could feel her resistance melting away. Intent on making her feel better, he swept aside her long blond hair, his hands drifting from her shoulders to the small of her back.

This close, it was impossible to ignore how attracted he was to her, and how much he longed to be even closer. So much closer. But they were in the middle of a room full of people. He needed to control himself.

"Don't stop," Morgan breathed, and even in the near darkness of the dance school's theater, it was easy to see the effect his touch had on her. Her eyes were half-closed, her limbs loose and relaxed, her lips parted as her soft breaths came slightly faster.

Seeing her like that—and knowing it was because of him—switched on a bright, hot light deep inside of him. He'd been trying to be so careful. Trying not to rush things, but now...

Brian slid his hands from her shoulders up to the nape of her neck, and when she turned toward him, he did what he'd wanted to do for seven long years and kissed her. Finally kissed her with all the hunger, all the pent-up need that he couldn't possibly hold back anymore.

Brian expected Morgan to pull back, but instead she kissed him back with the same intensity. Her fingers twined with his as they made out in the darkness, pulling each other so close that she was nearly on his lap and he was barely a breath from dragging her there.

The lights for intermission came up so

suddenly that they both jumped in shock. And as the light spilled over them so that he could see clearly into her eyes again, Morgan pulled away.

"Oh God, we shouldn't have—" She put her fingers over her lips. "Your students might have seen—" She shook her head as she stood up to flee.

Morgan's sister Emily was looking up at them, her expression impossible to read. But even though he worked with Emily at the high school, right then he didn't care what she was thinking. Morgan was the only one who mattered.

And she was slipping away.

Literally, given that when he went to follow her, several of his students' parents stopped him to chat about their kids' progress in his science class. By the time he was able to make his escape without being completely rude, he found that Morgan had taken Michael's seat in the front row next to Emily. Michael headed to the back of the theater to take Morgan's old seat next to Brian just as the lights began flashing to let the audience know they should return to their seats.

Michael was a few years older, but because Brian had dated Morgan for so many years in high school, he felt he knew the other man pretty well. Plus, he'd seen Michael with Emily enough times to recognize unrequited love when he saw it.

"Are you planning on starting things up with Morgan again?" Michael asked point-blank.

Brian appreciated the direct approach. "I'd

like to, yes."

"Morgan is like a sister to me, and her father won't have this talk with you, because he isn't that kind of guy, but I will." Michael pinned Brian with a hard gaze. "Don't hurt her."

"Hurting Morgan is the last thing I ever want to do."

Michael studied him in silence for a few moments before he finally nodded and turned his attention back to the two Walker women who were leaning in close and whispering to one another. Probably about the two of them.

"It's hard, isn't it?" Brian asked. "Wanting something that you know you might never be able to have, but not being able to stop wanting it despite that."

Michael didn't deny it or try to say that he didn't know what Brian was talking about. Instead, as he stared down at the back of Emily's head, Michael agreed, "Yes, it's hard."

CHAPTER TWELVE

After the performance, Morgan went straight home without speaking to Brian again. Grams, Paige and Emily came in a bit later, while Rachel and Charlotte had gone back to their own house.

Despite having run a major island performance tonight, Ava didn't seem to be tired at all as she bustled about, putting together a plate of homemade cookies for everyone. Emily made a pot of tea, while Paige looked over the digital pictures of the performance.

Morgan sat at the kitchen table and booted up her laptop to deal with her overflowing email inbox. Unfortunately, after a few minutes she realized she wasn't going to make much of a dent in her email, not when she couldn't stop thinking about Brian...and the kisses they'd shared tonight.

Kisses that she'd wanted to go on forever and

forever.

Kisses that were even sweeter than they'd been in her memory.

“Morgan?” Emily waved her arms in the air. “Earth to Morgan.”

She looked up from her computer screen. “Hmm?”

“I asked if you want tea.”

“Yes, please.”

When Grams sat down opposite her, Morgan said, “The performance tonight was great.”

“It was,” her grandmother agreed. “Paige is so good with the students.”

Paige smiled at the compliment, but said, “I just give them the tools to work it out for themselves and maybe point them in the right direction a couple of times when they get stuck.”

“You always make it sound easier than it is,” Morgan said, smiling at her soft-spoken sister. “But, seriously, my hat's off to both of you. I really had a great time watching the performance tonight.”

“I’m glad to hear it,” Ava said. “Although I did wonder why you switched seats partway through.”

Morgan had been hoping that no one but Emily would notice and try to give her advice. After all, she’d been ignoring well-meaning advice from her big sister all her life. But Grams was a different matter.

Ava held her own counsel much of the time

and usually let them figure things out for themselves...which meant that when she *did* offer advice, it was impossible to ignore. In fact, Morgan sometimes felt like she'd been able to leave the island only because Grams hadn't spoken out against it. Morgan suspected that Ava had even talked to her father, letting him know just how much Morgan needed to be set free to find her own way.

"It was nothing, Grams," she said, but every syllable she spoke was clearly a big fat lie. One that she hadn't been trying to tell herself for just three days, but for seven years.

"Now, Morgan," Ava said, "it's obviously *something,* especially since I can see that you're upset. What is it, dear? What had you running down to sit with your sister halfway through the show like that?"

Morgan knew there was no point in trying to pretend anymore when her grandmother and two sisters already seemed to know what she was trying not to tell them. "It's Brian." She lifted her hand to her lips without thinking. "He kissed me. Or I kissed him." She shook her head, as confused by it all as she'd ever been. "I honestly don't know how it happened, just that it did." And that she hadn't wanted it to stop. *Not ever.* "I'm so confused."

"Trust me," Grams said with a small smile, "if there's one thing I've learned from helping to raise you girls, it's that things are often simpler than you think."

"But it isn't simple!" she protested. "I shouldn't have kissed him. Not like that."

Emily and Paige gave each other a look, obviously trying to assess what being kissed *like that* meant exactly. But Grams didn't seem at all shocked by the idea that one of her granddaughters had been getting hot and heavy in the back of her dance studio with a former boyfriend.

"Now, what is so wrong about you kissing Brian? Don't you like the boy?"

"He's not a boy anymore, Grams." And that was part of what was making it harder. He'd said it himself back at the bar. They weren't kids anymore. They were adults with real responsibilities...and hearts that could be too easily broken again. She couldn't just dismiss all this as being some childish infatuation, or just a fun fling while she was in town on business, however much she might wish to. "What's wrong is that it can't work. All of you know that I love being back on the island, but that doesn't mean I can stay."

"You always say this, that you can't stay," Emily said from over by the stove. "Why not?"

"Because this isn't where my life is."

"But it could be." Emily sat down at the table with them. "It was while you were growing up. What's so wrong about life on the island that you had to leave the first chance that you got?"

Back in the theater, when Emily had been the protective older sister, Morgan had thought that perhaps she might understand. Yet it was obvious that when it came to the island, Emily would *never* understand how she felt.

"You've never gotten it, have you?" Morgan asked her sister. "Why I left? Why I *needed* to leave?"

"Needed?" Emily retorted. "What was out there that you couldn't find here? What could possibly be in New York City that was worth leaving all of this behind?"

"My career. Endless possibilities and choices. The chance to make my dreams come true. Do you think I could have gotten any of that if I hadn't left the island?"

"Honestly, since you never tried to make your dreams come true here, I don't know what would have been possible. But haven't you ever wondered about all the things that you might have had if you'd stayed?"

"Like what?"

"Brian, for a start. He loves you, Morgan. He's always loved you. And if you ask me, now that I've seen you two together again, I think you still love him, too."

Morgan swallowed hard. She should have guessed that Emily would be building up to this...and that she wouldn't pull her punches. Not when her older sister cared so much about all of them and not when Emily was always so sure about what would make each of them happy.

"Everything I am today," Morgan said in what she hoped was a measured voice, "I am because I left the island."

But instead of calming down, Emily almost looked angry now. "Do you really think that going away made you someone different? Do you really believe that your life came from leaving all this behind? There are things you can't leave behind, Morgan, even though you seem to be pretty determined to try. If you ask me, you are who you are *because* of the island."

"That's enough, girls." Ava reached out to take both their hands. "Finding happiness isn't about where you live your life. Look at me. Who would have thought that I would find love on an island a ferry ride away from my original home in Seattle? It isn't the place that matters. It isn't even what you do. It's whether everything in your life adds up to make you happy. We each have our own path. One that will change from time to time. One that will likely be full of twists and turns. One that might not look like the right path to anyone else." Here, she looked at each of them again. "But that doesn't mean it isn't right for you. So long as you're happy, that's the only thing that matters."

It all sounded so simple when Grams put it like that. Morgan should just do what made her happy. And there was no question that Brian made her happy, along with so many parts of life on the island, especially being with her family and feeling like she was a part of nature all the time. Yet, off the island she had her successful, ever-growing career that made her happy too. If it were just a case of choosing between something that made her happy and something that made her unhappy, then the choice would be every bit as simple as Grams suggested. Instead, any way she looked at it, things were far more complicated than that.

Especially when Morgan could still feel the strong pulse of attraction that came just from being near Brian and the taste of his lips on hers lingered, too. Because for all her memories of being in love with him as a teenager, the past several days had shown her just how intense their love could be if she allowed them to let it grow from a night of heated kisses into something more.

But if the fall had been hard when they were teenagers saying good-bye, how much worse would it tear them apart now?

"I know this must be really hard for you," Paige said as she moved behind Morgan's chair and put her arms around her, "especially when things with Brian are all happening so fast again."

"I swear I didn't expect to come back home to work on this project and start kissing Brian Russell in the back row of a dark theater like we used to as kids." She had to laugh at herself. "It's just that whenever I'm near him, I can't seem to control the way I feel. And it..." It was hard to admit this to anyone else, especially herself. "It scares me. Feeling so much for him when I know it can't ever become something more."

"But what if it could?" Emily had to ask. "What if you feel that much for him because he really *is* your forever?"

Morgan just stared at her sister, shocked by how right the thought of *forever* felt. "Are you saying you think I should give us a chance again while I'm here this summer?" God, even as she said it, she wanted nothing more than to get into her little red convertible, head straight to Brian's house, and kiss and kiss and kiss him until her head was spinning and her knees were weak.

"Maybe," Paige said in a gentle voice before Emily could respond or Morgan could leap, "since you're going to be here for a while longer, the best thing would be to give yourself some space to see if things feel right and if you think you can find a way to have everything you want on the island...or if you don't think you can."

For all that Morgan suddenly longed to throw caution to the wind and give herself over to desire for one perfect night with Brian, she knew Paige was right. Because she'd never forgive herself if she lost control and gave in to an impetuous yearning that only ended up destroying them both in the end.

CHAPTER THIRTEEN

"It's starting to look really good out here," Natalie observed a couple of weeks later as they stood together in the garden and looked over what they'd accomplished so far.

Today they were working together to dig a small irrigation channel, and Morgan knew it would go well, especially since both of her interns' confidence had grown tremendously during the time they'd worked together. That wasn't the only thing that had grown during the past couple of weeks, however. Every day as the two teenagers worked to shape and tend the garden, Natalie would constantly stare at Tad when he wasn't looking, while he stole just as many secret looks at her.

It was so tempting to try to give Natalie advice. But how could Morgan do that when she had been doing her best to keep her distance from Brian, working the jobs that put her farthest from him in an earnest attempt to keep their relationship from progressing in a dangerous direction?

"It really is looking great," Morgan agreed. "In fact, I think it's finally time to start pulling together some samples to show to the press. Would you like to work with me on that?"

Natalie nodded eagerly. "Mr. Russell's going to be there, too, won't he, since we're going to use the school labs?"

Apparently, keeping away from him wasn't going to be that easy after all. Not that Brian had been making it easy anyway. Every day, he'd brought down a picnic for them to share, or picked out flowers that he knew Morgan would like, or came by with a delicious container of homemade sorbet made from the island's own berries. They were all small, sweet things...just like he always used to do for her when they were a couple in high school.

At the same time, he hadn't tried to kiss her again or insisted that they have another big talk. Maybe it was crazy, but that only made it harder for Morgan. He'd told her that he was going to fight for her, but she should have known better than to think she'd be able to predict his tactics and then sidestep them. Especially when he'd always known exactly how to knock her walls down and touch the deepest parts of her.

And, honestly, today it *really* didn't help that

he'd taken his shirt off to work on the irrigation ditches he and Tad were digging, Brian's muscles well defined and shimmering with sweat in the sun. Of course, that was right when he stopped digging and caught her drooling over him. His slightly cocky grin had her breath catching in her throat...and her entire body tingling head to toe.

No. She needed to keep her wits about her. Needed to keep her focus on her career and fulfilling her dreams of having her own makeup line and TV show. After all these years, she was so close that she couldn't be derailed now.

A few minutes later when the men had put away their tools and come over, Morgan said to Tad and Natalie, "You both have done really great work with the irrigation. What do you say we head into the lab for our final hour today?"

"Morgan is going to let us help her make some samples!" Natalie informed Tad in an excited voice.

His smile for the girl was so warm, and so sweet, that Morgan's heart melted as he said, "That's really great news, Natalie." He turned to Morgan. "Thanks again for including us in everything."

"I honestly couldn't have done this without you. All of you."

But even as she said it to mean Natalie, Tad *and* Brian, she couldn't quite bring herself to look directly at Brian...not when she was afraid of just how sweet and warm his gaze at her would be.

And how it would likely melt away what was left of the walls she was trying to keep up around her heart.

* * *

After they had each filled a small bag with wild flowers and berries, they went into the school's science lab, where Morgan explained, "Most of the time, chemistry lessons are about creating reactions. With makeup, though, we want to avoid those as much as possible, because we certainly don't want ingredients reacting once they hit the skin. Well, except in things like fake tans, where the active ingredient—"

"DHA," Natalie supplied helpfully.

"Yes, DHA is designed to react with the skin. For things like lipstick and eye shadow, though, we want the results to be as inert as possible, while looking, smelling and feeling wonderful." After she spent a few more minutes talking them through the most important elements of creating makeup, she said, "Now you try," then let them loose with a handful of ingredients and the science lab's equipment. Since her own efforts with the ingredients she'd been using as an example were currently nothing more than multicolored goop, she wasn't expecting them to come up with perfect sticks of makeup. That was what the professional scientists would take care of later. The point was to get them to understand the process.

"You're good with them," Brian said as they watched the kids work.

"Thanks." She was surprised to find how much she enjoyed it. "So are you."

Their gazes held, and she forgot how to breathe, forgot everything except how hard her heart was beating, and how much she wanted Brian to pull her into his arms to kiss her again, and how—

"Morgan?"

"Brian?" She was already moving closer, could practically feel his arms around her again, when she finally realized why he was saying her name...and looking down at her bag.

Her phone was ringing.

Feeling like an idiot for practically jumping into his arms in the middle of his science lab with two of his students just feet away, she turned away as she put her phone to her ear.

"Juliet, hi." God, she needed to stop sounding so pathetically out of breath from nothing more than just being near Brian. *Focus.* She needed to focus. "How's everything going at the office?"

"Very well. And how is everything going on your end?"

"The new seeds are sprouting, the legacy wild berries are tamed, and the wildflowers are blooming like crazy." She paused, realizing as she said the words aloud just how far they'd come. And how much she'd enjoyed working outside with her small but very enthusiastic crew. "It's looking amazing, actually. In fact, our setup is pretty much done."

How had the last weeks flown by so quickly? Too quickly...

"Perfect," Juliet said, "because I've had several reporters tell me that they'd like to get down to the island this weekend to grab interviews with you in the garden and take photos."

"This weekend? They already want to come see the garden?"

"I thought you'd be thrilled with this news," Juliet said.

Juliet was a great assistant for a whole host of reasons, among them that she could read Morgan's tone even when the words themselves shouldn't have meant much. Only, Morgan wasn't sure that she wanted her assistant to read between the lines today.

"I am thrilled," she replied. "It's just that I had been thinking we had another week before we got to that point. Maybe even two." Panic set in at the thought of leaving the island so soon, even though her whole life, up until now, all she'd ever wanted to do was leave Walker Island behind.

"Why would you want to wait? If everything is ready and in bloom, we should be putting in the big marketing push, especially while the journalists are so excited about it."

Juliet was right. Moving on to the next step made perfect sense. It was just that she'd thought she'd have more time to try to figure out things with Brian. To see him smile. To hear him laugh. To sit with him beneath the warm sunshine. And to pretend that it wouldn't all have to come to an end the way it had before.

Only, how could she explain that to Juliet? Especially when she could hardly explain it to herself, this incredible longing for Brian when she *knew* that things could never work out for them.

"This weekend is fine. I'll be ready."

Brian was watching her carefully as she disconnected the call then worked on getting photos of Natalie and Tad working over a Bunsen burner, their heads close together to post on her social networking channels.

After graduation, Natalie would likely go off to one of the top universities in the country and Tad would likely head off on a football scholarship to play for one of the best college teams in the country. Now that they'd finished setting up the garden, Morgan would hire local workers to keep it going and to ship the ingredients to the cosmetics research labs. As soon as she returned to the city to film her new series, these weeks on Walker Island would be nothing but a sweet memory of sunshine and the sea...and a man who would always know, better than anyone else, how to make her smile.

And *feel.*

She looked up and realized that Brian was staring at her with concern. "Is everything okay?

It seemed like that phone call upset you."

For a few seconds she couldn't get her brain to work, not when she truly was upset at the thought of leaving him so soon. "Thank you for helping me, Brian."

His eyes darkened further, and she knew why. Because her thank-you sounded like good-bye.

"I would do anything for you, Morgan. You know that."

She wanted to say: *Come with me to New York. I don't want to live without you. Not again. Not ever again.*

But she'd never forgive herself for taking him away from the island and the school and the students he adored and who needed him, just so that she wouldn't have to be alone while she chased her dreams. So she simply said, "I know," before turning to Natalie and Tad and saying, "You've done so much to help me with this project. It wouldn't have worked nearly as well, or been anywhere near as fun, without you."

"I've really enjoyed working with you, too," Natalie said. "I learned a lot."

Tad nodded. "I have, too."

"That means so much to me," Morgan said, and it did, enough that her throat was starting to clog up at the thought of having to say good-bye to all three of them soon, not to mention her sisters and Ava. "I've been wanting to find a special way to say thank you to all of you."

"You're already writing us letters of recommendation," Natalie pointed out.

"You've earned those recommendations with your hard work, but I want to thank you personally by taking everyone out to celebrate the garden's success. How does the Waterside Room sound?"

It was the most expensive restaurant on the island. One that, growing up, Morgan would have killed to get into. It seemed like the only place good enough to show just how grateful she was to her two interns, and besides, she wanted to give them an occasion to remember.

CHAPTER FOURTEEN

Morgan took her time getting ready for dinner. Twice now, she'd scrapped outfits as unworkable: Her first choice of dress had been far too formal, while the second attempt had looked more like she was going to a picnic rather than to dinner. What *was* the right look, then? Something simple but beautiful? The classic but flirty little black dress? Maybe with a delicate red shawl, but that meant altering her makeup again, and there were still shoes to decide on...

"You know, Morgan, dear," Grams said as she walked into the bedroom and saw the cyclone of clothes and shoes and makeup, "for someone trying hard not to attract Brian, you seem to be spending a lot of time getting ready for this."

"It's a fancy restaurant. I should look nice. And you *know* I've always taken forever to get ready to go out."

"But you don't usually change your mind about how you want to look. That's something you've always known. Who you are. And what you want."

Before she could reply—or admit to her grandmother that she was becoming more confused by the day about what she truly wanted, Brian or her career, the city or the island—the doorbell rang. Emily had already let Brian in by the time Morgan headed downstairs.

When she saw him, she paused on the middle step and just stared, because he looked *amazing* in a suit and tie. "You look great," she said, her voice doing that breathless thing she'd almost gotten used to hearing come out of her mouth around him.

"You're always so beautiful, Morgan." He clearly didn't care that her grandmother and sisters and Michael were all within hearing distance as he told her, "You've taken my breath away."

She couldn't get her feet to move, not when all she could think was, *Don't you know that you take mine away, too?*

He didn't say anything more, just moved up the steps to where she was standing on trembling legs and held out his hand for her. When she took it, she felt the sweet jolt of electricity run all the way through her, continuing even as they walked in silence out to his car.

Seeing her interns in the backseat, she had to

work really hard to pull herself together as she greeted them and complimented them on their outfits. Tad had cleaned up well in his suit, and Natalie looked wonderful, the slightly geeky would-be scientist left behind for the evening, revealing a radiant young woman.

It had been a few years since Morgan had been to the Waterside Room, but it was still a truly magnificent establishment. The single, long dining room had a view out over the ocean, the lights of Seattle visible in the distance, and there were candles on each table.

"Ms. Walker," the maître d' said, "it's such an honor to have you here tonight." At the same time, strangely, he looked a little worried as he added, "I'm terribly afraid, however, that I was not able to accommodate your request in full at such late notice."

She couldn't stop her face from falling. "You don't have a table for us?"

"We have two tables for two, but not one for all four of you." Despite how apologetic he obviously was, he also felt that he needed to remind her, "This *is* the most sought-after restaurant on the island."

"It's fine," Brian said. "We can split up."

"Split up," Morgan started to protest, "but—"

Brian nodded over to where Tad and Natalie were completely wrapped up in one another with Natalie laughing softly at something Tad said, while Tad's fingers tentatively brushed Natalie's arm.

"Okay," Morgan said, even as her heart raced at the thought of being alone with Brian at a romantic table for two. "Separate tables will be fine, thank you."

Once they were seated, Brian said, "You must go to places like this a lot in the city, don't you?"

"Not as often as people think. Mostly when I do, it's because some TV executive wants to impress someone, or a client is feeling generous." In other words, not because she was having dinner with an incredibly handsome man that she was desperate to kiss. Yes, there had been fancy dates in the city with other men, but those dates had never felt right, and there had never been that spark, that special connection.

Only with Brian.

"The zombie movie you worked on was on TV last night," Brian said.

"What did you think?"

"Honestly? The makeup was great. But the acting?" He grinned and told her, "It almost turned me into a brainless zombie myself."

Morgan laughed, loud enough that a few people turned to see what was so funny. Generally, people in the industry were either careful about saying how great everyone's latest projects were or were tearing them apart out of jealousy. Whereas Brian had simply given her his honest—and funny—opinion. She'd always loved that about him.

She still did.

They talked about an email he'd gotten from his mom about a man she was dating, about his work at the high school, about her sisters and grandmother, and then, before Morgan knew it, their appetizers were removed and their main courses were being set down. The meal seemed to be passing by in the blink of an eye. Just her and Brian sitting close to one another while she listened to his voice in the soft twilight of the restaurant, never wanting the perfect evening to end.

She was getting sucked in again. Wanting to be with him all the time. Wanting to feel his arms around her. Wanting to be able to lean in to kiss him without ever having to stop.

"Ms. Walker, Mr. Russell, I'm sorry to interrupt, but I wanted to be sure to give you the check for both of your tables."

Morgan looked up at the waiter in surprise. "But we haven't even finished our main courses."

"I'm sorry, but I thought you might be in a hurry to get out of here."

That was when she looked up and realized all of the other diners were either standing up and putting on their coats to leave or had already left. "Why *is* everyone going so fast?"

He pointed out the window at the heavy rain that was blowing against the windows. "The fire department has issued a storm warning to all local businesses and residents. They're concerned about flash floods and would like everyone to get home safely as soon as possible."

When, Morgan wondered, had the faint drizzle turned into such a heavy, repetitive drumroll of water, sending water flooding down the glass? She'd been so engrossed in the storm of emotions that Brian had sent spinning inside of her that she'd never even noticed there was a storm raging outside, too.

"We should get the kids home before it gets worse," Brian said as he got up from the table then held out her chair for her to stand, too.

Morgan knew that she should have been terrified about what a storm like this would do to her newly planted garden and the damage it would surely do to the dream she had worked so hard to build up. But even after they'd dropped off the kids and Brian took her home, hugged her tight then told her everything was going to be okay before he went back to his own house, all she could think about was him.

CHAPTER FIFTEEN

At the first sign that the storm was letting up the next morning, Morgan headed for her garden. Emily had been in her element the previous night as the whole family had hunkered down in the house. She'd made soup for everyone while Michael had put on the storm shutters. Paige had worked on the choreography for a new student ballet in a section of the living room, while Rachel quoted the insurance statistics on storm damage. Fortunately, Charlotte hadn't been the least bit frightened of the storm as she had clapped her hands in excitement every time lightning flashed.

Morgan wished that she could feel even a tiny bit of the excitement from just days before. Instead, there was only a growing emptiness as she looked around the garden. The well-established berries had suffered some damage, but their roots and branches had been strong enough to withstand the storm. The newly planted garden, on the other hand, was a complete wreck. Plants had been uprooted by the wind and soil had been washed away by the rain so that it was barely more than a soupy mess of mud this morning.

Even worse? The reporters were coming tomorrow.

Morgan could only imagine the stories that they would come out with once they saw this. *Walker's Makeup Garden Fantasy Ends in Disaster*. She would look like a celebrity idiot who didn't know what she was doing, and it could potentially end this new phase of her career before it had even really begun.

There were a dozen soil and planting specialists she could have called to come consult with her on what could possibly be done, but the only person she wanted to call was Brian.

Yes, she knew her family would be there for her in a heartbeat, but right then he was the only one she wanted to see, the only one she needed to hold her tight and tell her that everything was going to be okay.

She had just pulled out her phone when she saw a big yellow school bus roll into view and park next to her red convertible. The doors opened, and she was shocked when Brian got off the bus. Natalie and Tad followed him...along with what looked like the entire high school football team. One by one, the teenage boys filed off the bus with tools and began working to put right the damage that the storm had inflicted.

Morgan couldn't believe her eyes as she turned from the huge group of working boys to Brian's gorgeous face. "You convinced the entire football team to help repair my garden?"

"Good morning, beautiful." Brian reached up to brush the back of his hand gently over her cheek. "Once I told them what happened, they were eager to help."

When she could finally manage to tear her gaze away from him, she was amazed by how quickly they were actually making progress. Not only were they all young men in good shape and eager to work hard, but there were so *many* of them, too! What had looked impossible just a few short minutes ago was already starting to take shape before Morgan's eyes, and suddenly she believed that they might actually succeed at repairing the garden in time for the reporters' visit.

Natalie moved up and down the lines of the football team like a general inspecting her troops, helping out occasionally with some of the work, but mostly issuing instructions on what each person needed to do to get the garden back in shape.

As Brian moved to help deal with a patch where several brambles had blown together and created a wall of thorns, Natalie came to stand beside Morgan. "Jocks aren't all bad, are they?"

"If you ask me," Morgan said, her eyes overflowing with grateful tears as she watched Brian and his team work so hard to save her dream, "they're absolutely amazing."

* * *

After a lifetime of football practices and games, Brian was used to spending plenty of time in the mud, but today had taken *dirty* to a new level. He felt as if the mud had dug its way so deep into his skin that the scalding heat of the shower was barely enough to wash it away.

And he'd do it all over again tomorrow, just for the pleasure of seeing the look on Morgan's face when he'd shown up with the team.

He'd been so impressed with the way his team had risen to the occasion. He'd expected some of them to complain or refuse, to say that they were there for football practice rather than gardening. Yet none of them had. It felt good knowing that they trusted him enough to help just because he'd asked. It felt even better knowing that he'd been able to help Morgan with something that meant so much to her.

After drying off and putting on a pair of sweatpants, Brian had just settled down to work through the video from last weekend's game when he heard a knock on the door. He looked around for a T-shirt to throw on, but when he heard a familiar voice say his name, he forgot all about needing to put on more clothes and hurried over to open up the door.

Morgan looked so beautiful standing on his front step in a colorful summer dress that he actually lost his breath.

“Can I come in?” she asked. Brian caught the flicker of her eyes over his body...and the heat that immediately flared in them. “I didn’t catch you at a bad time, did I?”

Since when did they have to ask one another things like that, he thought as he stepped aside to let her in. With her, there *was* no bad time.

“I wanted to come by and say thank you.” She sounded a little nervous, though, more nervous than someone would have been if they really were there only to say thanks. “What you did for me today...I’m just *so* grateful. You completely saved my makeup line, because now when the reporters come tomorrow, they won't have any reason to crucify me and my big dreams.”

“It wasn’t just me,” Brian said, even though a part of him would have loved to take all of the credit and make it just about him and Morgan. “Your family would have done the same. Most people on the island would have.”

“But they didn't. *You* did.” Morgan started to move closer to him, before stopping her progress. “Being back here on the island, being around you so much, and then after what you did for me today...” She shook her head, and he could read the confusion on her face. “There have been so many emotions going around and around in my head that I haven't known what to think."

"Are you sure you haven't known what to think?" Brian asked, closing the final distance between them. "Tell me, how have you felt since you've been back? Since we've gotten to see each other again every day?"

"Happy." She looked more than a little surprised by the one short word that she'd blurted out, but a few seconds later she was saying, "I've been really, really happy. You, my family, the island...everything has been so good since I got back here." But then she frowned and added, "It's just—"

Brian put a finger to her lips. "You don't have to make things complicated, Morgan."

"Things *are* complicated. We both know that," she insisted, but she fortunately didn't move away from him.

And as she met his gaze straight on and let him see into her extraordinarily beautiful blue eyes, he asked her, "Do you want to kiss me, Morgan?"

She didn't hesitate, didn't look confused at all anymore, as she said, "Yes."

"Then take what you want, Morgan. Don't you know it's one of the things I've always loved most about you?"

Each word from his lips was husky and full of not only need but love. So much love that when she moved fully into the circle of his arms and lifted hers to twine around his neck, he nearly fell to his knees in gratitude.

And then, thank God, her lips were pressing against his. Oh, how he loved the sweet press of her curves against him, the passion that grew as he kissed her back, holding her tightly against him while her hands roamed over him and she made little sounds of soul-deep pleasure.

Morgan pulled back briefly, looking at him as though searching for something, and for a moment he thought she might have changed her mind about being with him. But then, thankfully, she smiled and said, “I’ve just realized I don’t know the way to your bedroom.”

He kissed her again then, over and over and over, until it didn't matter where his bedroom was because neither of them could make it any farther than the living room couch to strip away each other's clothes and love each other.

CHAPTER SIXTEEN

For a few moments after she woke, Morgan couldn't place where she was. Not at her family's home on the island. Not in New York, either, or one of the innumerable hotels she was always staying in. But then the scent of French toast floated to her from the kitchen, and she finally remembered.

Brian. He'd always made the most delicious French toast.

She hugged his pillow to her, loving the way it smelled like him, a clean masculine scent that shot all of her hormones to rising again. Last night had been *amazing.* She'd thought she'd remembered how good it had been between them in high school but...oh my...the way he'd touched her, the way he'd kissed her, the way he'd loved her last night! It had been so good that she could still hardly believe it was possible to feel that much pleasure. That much bliss. Joy that seemed to go on and on forever and ever.

The previous morning, standing in her ruined garden after the storm, she'd felt devastated, as it had seemed that her plans for her makeup line had all washed away. But then Brian had come to help with his students like a white knight with an army of squires. All for her, to support her dreams, just the way he always had.

It had been so natural, so obvious, to go to Brian after that. To stop denying the attraction that had only grown bigger and bigger between them since she'd returned to the island. To push away her doubts for a little while and give in to hours of loving and being loved by the most wonderful, beautiful man in the world.

When the smell of bacon mingled with the French toast, her growling stomach insisted she get out of the bed. A short while later she found Brian in the kitchen with the sunlight from the window spilling over him. Morgan stood in the doorway for a moment or two, before she stepped close enough to wrap her arms around him from the back. Laying her head against him, she loved listening to the steady beat of his heart.

"I thought French toast might be enough to wake even you up," Brian said as he turned and kissed her, his mouth sweet and gentle—and utterly delicious—against hers. He popped a piece into her mouth, and when she moaned her pleasure, he said, "Would you like more?"

"Of the toast or of you?"

"How about both?"

Brian looked so tempting that it was almost impossible not to drag him back into the bedroom. Yet a quick glance at the clock on the wall told Morgan that, unfortunately, she couldn't.

"I actually have to skip both," she said with palpable regret. "I'm running late already."

"Are you sure whatever it is can't wait just a little while?" Brian asked as he pressed a kiss below her earlobe

Morgan shivered at the sensual pleasure of his mouth on one of her most sensitive spots. "I think we both know that if we go there, neither one of us will get anything else done today."

"You say that like it's a bad thing."

His teeth scraped across her earlobe, and she let out a little gasp at how good it felt. *More.* She wanted *more.* Which was why she needed to remind them both that, "I need to meet with Natalie this morning and then I've got all those interviews with the reporters at the garden this afternoon." She tilted her head to smile up at him. "After all the work you put in yesterday, I want to make sure they know who made it all possible."

Brian brushed his fingertips lightly across her lower lip. "I didn't do it for them."

No, he'd done it to make *her* happy. And that was exactly how she felt when she'd been with him last night. Happy. Safe. And calm for the first time in a very long time, like she didn't have to keep running as fast as she could just to keep up.

"What do you have planned with Natalie?" Brian asked.

"She'd like to tour some universities in New York, and I was going to give her a few tips on places to stay, along with some activities and groups to check out while she's there. After all she's done here for me, the least I can do is help her plan properly so that she can get the most out of the experience."

"She's lucky that she's got you to help her."

"And you as her teacher. Although," Morgan added, "since I still don't have anywhere near all the answers, a part of me wonders how much I can really help."

"A lot," Brian said, with utter certainty. "Besides, lately I've been thinking that maybe we don't have to have everything planned. Maybe sometimes it's enough to just go with what we feel."

She knew he was waiting for her to agree, but when she remained silent, instead of pushing her, he simply said, "How about I make you dinner tonight to celebrate your successful press interviews and the official public launch of your new venture?"

"I'd love that, and if you wanted to make me breakfast-for-dinner so that I can really enjoy your French toast and bacon, I probably wouldn't complain."

"With all the naps you take," Brian said with

a smile as he continued to hold her close, "it's no surprise that breakfast is the only meal that you're ever in the mood for considering you've always just woken up."

He had a point. Especially since as she stood there in Brian's kitchen, on the island where she'd been born and raised, Morgan suddenly felt like a part of her that she hadn't known about before had finally woken up, too.

* * *

Morgan barely had time to shower and change before Natalie came by her house. From the extremely curious and speculative way that Emily and Paige looked at Morgan when she walked into the living room, it was obvious that Natalie's presence was the only thing stopping them from asking for all the juicy details. She'd texted the night before to let them know that she wouldn't be coming home because she was staying with Brian, but had left the rest of it up to their imaginations.

Morgan showed Natalie through to the living room where she opened her laptop and pulled a map of New York out of her bag. Emily came in just long enough to ask if they wanted coffee, and it seemed to catch Natalie a little by surprise, realizing that her school guidance counselor was a normal person like anyone else.

"What we need for you," Morgan said, "are hotels that are going to be affordable for your family while still being in a nice part of town."

"Is New York that dangerous?" Natalie asked, and Morgan realized that since the biggest city Natalie had ever been to was Seattle, as exciting as all the opportunities in front of her seemed, they were also pretty frightening, too.

"There are some dangerous parts, but where you'll be touring, you really just need to know where you're going and pay attention. Somewhere in Prospect Heights might work for a place to use as your home base." Morgan drew a circle on the map. "I'm just sorry I don't have the room to put you up when you come to visit." As nice as her apartment was back in New York, it was still only a one-bedroom walkup.

So different from this house on the island, Morgan thought as she heard the door open and Rachel come in with Charlotte. Her cute little niece would no doubt demand to be allowed to help her aunt once she saw that she was drawing on maps. Morgan could also hear the faint sounds of Emily debating something with Michael, which meant that he must have come around to fix something again. Paige chimed in every once in a while, and Grams was probably down at the dance studio. Yet, the house still seemed to have enough room in it for everyone to have their own space when they wanted it.

Until she'd come back this summer, Morgan hadn't realized how much she missed having her family around her while still having the space to do all that she needed to do. When Morgan had been younger, she'd worried that returning to the island would feel like being trapped. However, now that she'd spent several weeks here, she realized it hadn't been like that at all. The others weren't trying to trap her, they were supporting her. Especially Brian.

So then, why had she always believed she needed to run from them all?

Morgan looked back down at the map. "There are so many things to see in this neighborhood, and the restaurants are just great." She smiled at Natalie. "You must be so excited about all this. You have *such* a bright future ahead of you."

Morgan could see the girl's future laid out as clearly as the map was. College, summer internships, postgraduate work, all leading up to a job doing anything she wanted. Whatever Natalie put her mind to, Morgan was sure that she would succeed even beyond their already tall expectations.

Natalie smiled at the compliment, but as she looked back down at the map, Morgan noticed that her smile had slipped a little.

"What is it, Natalie? What's wrong?"

The girl was silent for a few moments before she finally said, "It's kind of complicated, and you've already helped me so much with everything else."

"I know all about complicated," Morgan assured her. She'd left Brian's house a little while ago feeling warm and soft and dreamy, but looking at the New York City map and thinking about being back there soon had quickly brought back up every single one of her conflicting thoughts about Brian and the island. "Trust me, Natalie. Whatever it is, you can tell me, and I'll do my best to help you."

"It's just that I've been having these...these feelings. For Tad. I never thought that a guy like him would ever look twice at a girl like me, and I know this might sound bad, but I also kind of thought that he was just some dumb jock. The thing is, he's not. He's so sweet, and good-looking, and he listens so well. He's smart, too." She looked really distraught over it all. "I don't know what to do. Not like I used to. Not like I always have."

The answer should have been obvious. Morgan should have been telling Natalie that Tad was sweet, but with the future she had lined up ahead of her, she couldn't afford to let it all fall by the wayside for a boy. Morgan should have been telling her that leaving him behind was the hard thing to do, but that sometimes the hard thing was the *right* thing.

The problem was...Morgan could still feel not only the brush of Brian's hands and mouth over her skin, and the pure, sweet joy of being with him, but also how badly she wanted to be with him again, safe and warm in his arms.

If Natalie had asked her this question when

Morgan had first come to the island, the answer would have been simple. She would have told Natalie to go forward in the direction of her big dreams and not look back, because she would find everything she wanted, including someone to love, out there in the world. Yet did it ever actually work like that? Because if she were being completely honest with herself, Morgan had never actually found anyone, or anything, to replace the only person she'd ever really loved. A truly incredible man who had come to mean more to her with every moment she'd spent with him these past few weeks.

"What's more important?" Natalie asked as Morgan's brain spun in circles. "Is it my career? Is it everything I've got lined up and all of my dreams? Or is it Tad? Because I think I love him, Morgan."

Morgan felt utterly out of her depth, but then suddenly she heard her grandmother's voice in her head. *"It isn't the place that matters. It isn't even what you do. So long as you're happy, that's the only thing that matters. But some things, I think, we've just got to figure out for ourselves."*

"I wish I could tell you what to do, Natalie, but the truth is that I've been asking myself the same questions. All I know is that whatever decisions we make, both of us need to be happy. Because that's the most important thing of all."

CHAPTER SEVENTEEN

A short while later, Morgan made sure her game face was on as the reporters approached. "Xander, Stephanie, I'm so glad you could make it. How was the trip over on the ferry?"

"Wavy," the female reporter replied, one hand over her stomach, clearly not someone with sea legs. "This is what has taken you away from the red carpet for the last few weeks?" The woman looked around the land as if she wasn't quite sure what to make of it. "Gardening?"

Morgan smiled at the group of reporters who had gathered around her. "As I'm sure my publicist told you, I will be launching my new makeover show soon. In conjunction with that, I will also be bringing out my own makeup line. Only, what I'm doing is about more than just wanting to see my name on lipstick cases." Morgan explained about the island, about her family's history, and about resurrecting the old Walker plot with the help of local students.

"Are you saying that you've come back here in search of special ingredients you can't find elsewhere?" a reporter from the *Los Angeles Journal* asked.

"It's certainly true that the island's unique microclimate means it's good for growing a wide range of potential ingredients. But the magic ingredient is less about the varietals of berries that I'm growing and more about the love and attention that come from working with my family and friends and the entire community to get this garden growing again, the way it used to when the island was first founded. I've been thrilled to have had a great deal of success working as a makeup artist off of the island, but now I'd like to see if I can bring the island back in via Walker Cosmetics."

As if on cue, Brian's car pulled up next to the reporters' rental cars. "In fact, here is my team of helpers right now. This is Brian Russell, the school's science teacher and football coach, along with Tad Burrows and Natalie Fields, who have done great jobs as my interns. Perhaps I could give everyone a tour of the garden first, and then we can divide up so that you can all get the interviews you need?"

None of which was what Morgan wanted to do right then. Not when every cell in her body was urging her to rush over to Brian and kiss him.

No, she reminded herself, *you need to focus on the reporters and on your career that you've worked so hard to build.* But even as she worked to focus, she couldn't help but wonder, *What about love? When does that get to come first?*

Fortunately, Brian was the one who stepped in to help shift her focus back to the job at hand by beginning the tour of the garden. A few minutes later he deftly passed it off to her so that she could explain how the four of them had mixed in new, sustainable plants with the legacy plants that had already been in the plot. She showed them the "before" pictures of the plot to show just how much work had gone into transforming the garden. And when a few of them questioned whether she'd actually gotten her fingernails dirty working in the garden or if she'd simply overseen her crew while *they* got dirty, she rolled up her sleeves and showed them where the brambles had cut into her skin. She didn't take offense at their disbelief. It wasn't their world, so they naturally assumed it wasn't hers, either.

Because they think I'm one of them. A part of their same world of celebrities and fashion advice, red carpets and premieres.

Only, she'd grown up in this garden and on the water all around the island, and the truth was that it was as much a part of her as the glitz and glamour of working on movies.

As the reporters drank the fresh raspberry lemonade that she'd made for them and the sun shone down over the island, making everything around them positively glow, Morgan knew the scene couldn't have been more PR perfect. She should have been rejoicing that everything had come together even better than she'd hoped it would. And yet...it was so hard to keep playing this game in which she was acting like she had it all together and knew exactly what she was doing, when she felt pulled into two completely different directions on the inside.

Morgan had done enough interviews to be able to confidently make it through the rest of the afternoon with the reporters, but every few questions, she couldn't help but look across the garden at Brian, if only to reassure herself that he was still there. Each time he smiled back at her, her heart beat just a little harder, just a little faster.

Finally, the reporters got everything they needed and left to catch the ferry back to the mainland. Natalie and Tad left shortly after that.

"What's wrong?" Brian asked when they were finally alone again.

She wanted so badly to step into his arms and just let him hold her, but she knew she first had to share with him what she was feeling. "Natalie asked me a question earlier today that I haven't been able to stop thinking about. She wanted me to tell her what was more important—her career or what she feels for Tad?"

Brian's gaze was steady on hers as he asked,

"What did you tell her?"

"I should have told her to follow her dreams. I should have told her to be brave and go out into the big wide world after what she wants so that she can become everything that she's meant to be. It's the right advice."

"Is it?"

"It's what I did. If I hadn't gone, I wouldn't have any of what I have now. I wouldn't have my successful career or my upcoming makeup line. I wouldn't have a makeover show with a major network." So why hadn't she been able to say that to Natalie?

"I agree," he surprised her by saying. "You wouldn't have any of those things if you hadn't left the island. But you didn't say any of that to her?"

"I told her that I didn't know what the answer was. Why would I do something like that? I *hate* that I was so wishy-washy when she was looking to me for advice. I hate..."

"What do you hate, Morgan?"

"I hate how confused I feel about everything. I hate that things aren't crystal clear the way I used to think they were. I have everything I thought I ever wanted. A thriving career. A big bank account. Fame. You know how you hear about these celebrities who have the nerve to be unhappy with their lives?" She made a face. "I *should* be happy. I should be ecstatic. And for seven years, I've thought that I was. But ever since I came back to the island, it feels like everything has shifted around under me. I shouldn't feel like I'm falling apart because"—*because of you*—"just because I've come back. But this is what the island always does to me!" And what *he* did to her. Because when she was around Brian, nothing else seemed to matter.

Brian stepped closer to her and cupped her cheek as he stared deeply into her eyes. "I love you, too."

He knew she loved him? But, of course, he knew. He'd always known exactly what was inside her heart, way back to when they were just a little girl and boy out on the playground.

As he wiped away her tears, she knew this was the moment of reckoning, the one where she'd have no choice but to throw away everything she'd worked so long and hard to build because she couldn't imagine leaving him.

But even though he'd just declared his love for her, he didn't look the least bit happy as he gazed down at her. On the contrary, the man she loved looked like his heart was breaking into a million pieces.

"I love you so much that I can't actually do it," he told her in a raw, hollow voice. "Even though I thought I could. Even though I've been telling myself for weeks that I would do it. That I would do whatever I needed to do to make you stay, no matter what, this time. That I would convince you that you'd done enough in the city and had enough success to be happy staying here on the island with me now."

Her heart had all but stopped beating in her chest by the time she whispered, "What are you saying, Brian?"

"I told you I wouldn't let you go again, but I know how important your dreams, and your career, are to you. Because they're just as important to me. All I want is for you to be happy. It's all I've ever wanted."

"I am happy with you," she told him, the deepest truth she knew.

And yet, even after she'd said the words, Brian closed his eyes tight for a few seconds before opening them again and searing her with the intensity of his gaze. "If you stayed today, if you didn't get on that plane back to New York, do you think you could continue to be happy? Or would you eventually end up resenting me, and your family, and the entire island for holding you back from achieving the rest of your dreams?"

Back in high school, she'd known for sure that she needed to leave or she'd regret it all her life. But now? Now things weren't nearly as cut-and-dried. She loved Brian, loved her family, loved always being so close to nature on the island. But her career was almost entirely based in New York. Maybe if she'd had another week or two to try to figure things out, she'd have a clear solution all mapped out.

"This was why I tried to keep my distance

from you," she said. "I didn't want this to happen again, for us to have to say good-bye. But I couldn't stay away." She couldn't stop her tears from falling. "I'm sorry I couldn't stay away."

"Even if you can't stay, every moment I got to spend with you," he said as he pulled her into his arms and held her close one more time, "was worth it."

CHAPTER EIGHTEEN

"How is your packing going, dear?" Grams asked from the doorway to Morgan's room.

"Everything fit in the case when I came here," she said, frowning as she looked at the huge pile of clothes and shoes and makeup that wouldn't even come close to zipping into her suitcase.

"I find that's the way with things," Ava said as she came into the room to help. "They never fit as neatly as we might like."

"Can you make sure that the others get the bag of makeup?" Morgan asked, nodding to one of the many things she was going to have to leave behind. "I'm sure it will suit them." Morgan finally got her suitcase closed, then moved to hug her grandmother. "I really loved being back here, Grams."

"You know you're welcome back anytime. Perhaps you won't leave it so long next time?"

But Morgan wasn't sure how realistic it was to start thinking about coming back home again. After all, she'd barely managed to get back to the island in the past seven years, and with her own TV show and makeup line, things were hardly likely to get any less busy.

Morgan checked her watch and knew she needed to get going to make her flight. And yet, she wasn't quite ready to go. Not when she still felt so churned up inside. "Grams?"

"Mmm?"

"I—" A thousand thoughts jumbled into her brain, but the only one that came out was, "I'm nervous."

"About what?"

"About making the wrong choice."

Morgan expected her grandmother to tell her everything would be okay and that she would support her no matter what choice she made. Instead, Ava patted the bed and gestured for them to sit down side by side.

"Back when I was a professional dancer, I knew all about putting on a face for a show. But one of the things I loved most about transforming into someone else while on stage was getting to take it off afterward and become *me* again." She reached for Morgan's hand. "The worst nights were when it felt like I needed to leave it on. Not just the makeup, but the mask." Grams brushed a lock of hair away from Morgan's face, and for a moment she felt more like a fifteen-year-old girl than a full grown woman. "Sometimes when I look at you, I see a beautiful young woman who doesn't *know* how beautiful she is. How beautiful she has *always* been."

"Are you sure you don't have me mixed up with Paige, Grams?" Morgan tried to tease to lighten the moment. One that felt truly overwhelming. "She's the one who never lets me make her over."

"Whereas you've made over your whole life. Even though you have always been perfect just as you are."

The kitchen clock chimed downstairs. "Grams"—Morgan was horribly choked up—"I have to go or I'll miss my flight."

Downstairs, she hugged Emily, Rachel, Paige and Charlotte good-bye—her heart in her throat the entire time—then drove down to the docks and returned her rental car before boarding the ferry. Brian hadn't come to say good-bye, and she knew why. If he'd been there, she never would have gotten on the ferry...and he loved her too much to do anything that could destroy her career. But, God, she missed him *so badly* that even as she stood at the rail of the ferry in the fresh air, she could barely get any oxygen into her constricted lungs.

In the airport lounge, she had just enough time to scroll through the links Juliet had emailed her for the stories the reporters had written about her garden. It seemed that the idea of her all-natural makeup line and its ties to home had struck a chord with them. Even better, the readers' initial responses to her having her own makeover show indicated that it could be a big hit. Digesting the details, Morgan could already feel herself starting to slip back into the world of ratings and opinions, executives and urgent meetings. A world away from the island, her family, and the garden.

And, most of all, a world away from Brian.

"Excuse me?"

Morgan looked up at a girl in her late teens. "Are you Morgan Walker? I've seen your segments on the morning news, and I was wondering...can anyone apply to have a makeover on your show or are there special rules?"

Morgan considered the girl for a moment or two. She was already very pretty, although perhaps she could do with a couple of tips on how to apply eye shadow so that it didn't dominate everything else.

"How about if we try a mini-makeover right here?" She didn't have much makeup with her, but the girl had a fairly full bag of products. A short while later, Morgan asked, "How's that?"

The girl, who'd said her name was Vicky, looked in a mirror and frowned. "I don't look any different."

"That's because you are *already* beautiful, Vicky," Morgan said to the clearly disappointed girl. "Trust me, this is a very good look for you."

"But I still look like *me.* Well, me with less makeup than usual, anyway."

"Yes, you do," Morgan said with a smile. "And I, for one, am really proud to have helped make you over into the wonderful, beautiful person you already are."

Finally, the girl smiled back. "Thanks, Morgan. I didn't know you could do that, but now that you've put it that way, I guess this *is* a really good makeover."

It really was, Morgan thought as the call for her flight came and she hugged her new friend good-bye. All the while she was thinking back to being seventeen and wanting the same kind of massive makeover that Vicky had asked for. Not just her hair or makeup, but her *entire life.* And it was exactly what she'd done by transforming herself from a small-town island girl into someone who could confidently walk into any boardroom in New York City or Hollywood and feel at home.

And yet, now that she was leaving again, she wasn't sure that her real home had ever really been anyplace other than Walker Island...

* * *

Emily ran into Michael as she came around the corner into the kitchen. He caught her firmly in his arms, and she was about to snap at him when she stopped herself. "Sorry." She made herself step out of his warm—and incredibly strong—arms. "I was just heading out to yank some weeds in the garden. They've been growing so fast, and every time I look out the window into the backyard, it drives me crazy to see how they're crowding out all the flowers."

"I miss Morgan, too," he said gently, letting go of everything except her hand, which he held for a beat longer than he needed to.

"She's only just gone," Emily said. "I shouldn't be missing her already."

"I always start missing her even before she's gone," Paige admitted as she moved down the hall past them in her dance gear. She didn't have to open up the studio for an hour, but when she was upset she always turned to dancing to try to make herself feel better. "But somehow that doesn't make it hurt any less once she actually leaves."

Just then Rachel came down the stairs with Charlotte in her arms, saying, "I'm not going to go anywhere, honey. I promise."

"But Aunt Morgan did," Charlotte insisted.

"Morgan has to go to work in New York."

"But I want her here. Why can't she stay on the island with the rest of us?"

How could Rachel begin to explain to her young daughter why her aunt needed to go all the way to New York to find what she needed? Especially when there was so much love for her here?

"Charlotte," Emily said, "how would you like to come help me make cupcakes?" But Charlotte shook her head as she remained in her mother's arms, clearly too bummed out for cupcakes. Nonetheless, Emily decided to forgo the weeds for the time being and make the cupcakes anyway. They would all be in need of comfort food tonight.

"I really thought we had her back this time," Emily said as she started to pull together the ingredients.

"Would you want to spend your time here if you got to spend it elbow to elbow with celebrities instead?" Michael asked.

"This is home." And it really was that simple to Emily. "Why would I want to be somewhere else?"

Grams came in with her computer, but put it down to coax Charlotte out of Rachel's arms. "Would you like to help me sort through my fan mail, sweetheart? You can help me type."

Of all of them, only Grams seemed happy. She was smiling as she went through her email with Charlotte on her lap, humming away to herself as she coached Charlotte to type words for her, one letter at a time.

"Grams," Emily said, "is everything all right?"

"Oh yes, everything's fine. Boy, setting up this Facebook page sure has increased the number of people who are contacting me every day. Joannie mentioned that she thought I should set up a Pinterest page, too, to post pictures of the island throughout the seasons."

"Maybe you should, Grams, but"—Rachel shot Emily a look—"are you sure you're okay?"

"Yes, I'm quite sure, girls. Why would you think that I'm not?"

"Well," Emily said, "you don't seem to be taking Morgan's leaving very hard."

"You're worrying that I might finally have gone cuckoo in my old age?" Ava asked. She lifted Charlotte down off her knee so the girl could run back to Rachel.

"No, it isn't that," Rachel assured her.

"Listen to me, girls. You don't need to worry about me. And you don't need to worry about your sister, either. These things work out."

"That's easy to say, but—" Emily stopped when she saw her grandmother shaking her head.

"I'm not just saying it to try to make myself, or you girls, feel better. I'm confident that things will work out exactly the way they should."

"How can you be so sure?"

Ava smiled at her granddaughters. "Because if there's one thing I believe in, it's true love."

CHAPTER NINETEEN

Morgan was just settling into her seat on the airplane when her phone went off. “I know you're about to take off,” Juliet said when she picked up, “but even though you saw the links I sent you to the amazing articles about your garden and upcoming makeup line, what I hadn't yet sent you was the *huge* amount of interest they've already generated in your social media streams. It’s just *exploded*. People love the pictures you posted of the garden. They love the story of you going back home to grow some of the ingredients. If even a quarter of the readers tune in for the first episode or try one of the products...this could be *huge*, Morgan.”

“That’s great, Juliet.”

“Great? That's all you have to say when we’ve got national media coverage and we’ve just gone *viral*? I mean, pretty soon you aren’t going to be able to walk down the street without people recognizing you."

Juliet said that as though it was the most incredible thing in the world. But Morgan didn't see how it changed much. After all, for the last few weeks practically everyone had known who she was. Of course, that had just been on the island, but it was still more than enough.

Morgan found herself thinking about her sisters, about what they would be doing right now. Paige would be at the dance studio working with the students. Rachel would be playing with Charlotte. Hanna would probably be on the deck of one of Joel's boats filming something beautiful. Emily would be bustling around the house, baking and throwing sparks with Michael. Grams would be chatting online with all the fans she'd gotten after starring in Hanna's documentary.

And Brian? Well, he might be out on the football field with his players. Or maybe he would be walking over to her garden to keep an eye on it. Or maybe, just maybe, he was missing her so badly that he'd still be trying to take a full breath, the way she still was.

"Once you're back in the city, we'll need to get together to work out the details for the filming," Juliet said. "Most of them are already in place, but if they don't fit in with what you have in mind, I can probably get the studio to change them."

"I'm sure the schedule will be fine," Morgan said without really thinking about it. What would it feel like, being back in New York where she couldn't just walk everywhere like she could on the island? Where there were eight million people rather than a couple of thousand? Where Morgan didn't already know nearly everyone?

Where there wasn't Brian.

"Are you all right, Morgan?"

Morgan knew she needed to go back to New York because everything that she'd done, everything that she'd become, was there. And if she didn't go back, wouldn't it be the same as admitting that she'd made the wrong choice seven years ago when she'd left the island, and her family, and Brian, to make over her entire life?

"You never needed a makeover, darling."

Her grandmother's words came back to her then, but Juliet was still talking, and Morgan knew that she needed to pay attention since there was more to do than ever once she landed in New York.

"I'm in talks with a couple of the chat shows. As you know, once one of them agrees to book you, the others will, too."

"That's good," Morgan said absently.

"Before you go, I wanted to remind you that there's filming all week in the mornings, obviously, and then Monday afternoon is the meeting with the manufacturers about the makeup line. Tuesday, you have distributors and an interview for the radio, then in the evening..."

Her life was planned out like a military operation. There was no room in it for anything beyond meetings, and shooting, and makeup.

"Are you listening?" Juliet finally asked. "Seriously, Morgan, are you okay?"

Was she? Morgan should have been so eager to get back to New York and on to this big step up in her career. It was what she had worked toward for so long, the kind of fame and success for which she had left the island in the first place.

For which she'd left Brian seven years ago.

But now, as she sat there hearing about all the meetings and the filming sessions that were coming, she felt as if something was shriveling up inside her. As if a pit had opened up in her stomach and everything was being sucked down into it.

"You never needed a makeover."

"Ma'am, we're going to be shutting the doors in a minute," the flight attendant said. "I'm afraid you need to turn your phone off now."

Morgan had been so sure when she left as a kid that Walker Island had been holding her back. That it—and her family, friends, Brian—had been millstones around her neck, dragging her down as she tried to soar. It had taken these past three weeks for her to realize just how wrong she'd been.

"Morgan?" Juliet asked. "Are you still there?"

"Ma'am," the flight attendant said in a far sterner voice than she'd used before, "you really have to finish your call now. I'm sure that whatever it is, it will still be there when we land."

But that was just the problem. It wouldn't be. Because chances were like bubbles floating on the breeze. They could burst at any moment. Of course, there was another side to that analogy. Go after them too hard, grab at them with both hands, and everything truly worth having could burst.

What did she want?

It was the question she'd been asking herself all week, but hadn't been able to answer. But now that she'd actually left again, she suddenly knew, based on how wrong it felt—and how unhappy she was—that she was making the wrong decision.

Yes, she wanted great success with both her makeup line and new show, but she also wanted her family. She wanted her friends. She wanted the island.

And, most of all, she wanted Brian and his love.

New York, she already knew, couldn't give her all that. It had given her some things, but not enough. Not nearly enough.

"Ma'am, if you don't turn that cell phone off," the flight attendant said in a really stern voice, "I'm going to have to call security."

"That's fine," Morgan said as she grabbed her bag and stood up. "I'm not going to be taking this flight after all. Could you arrange for my bags to be taken off the plane, please?"

"What? But we're almost ready to take off."

"Yes, I know. That's why I have to get off the plane."

It had taken her this long to finally see that Walker Island hadn't been holding her back. On the contrary, it had always given Morgan things she couldn't get anywhere else. A place where she belonged. A big family that was always there for her. And Brian.

Always Brian.

Yes, she'd had to leave for a few years to get the other half of what she wanted, but that was the point. What lay in New York was only half of what Morgan wanted in her life, and not even the most important half.

Without the most important half, it just didn't make sense.

"Juliet," Morgan said into her phone as she headed for the exit of the plane, "you know how you've been pretty much running things while I've been here?"

"You're not coming back, are you?"

"I'll get flights over when I absolutely need to film in New York, but no, I'm not coming back to live and work in New York. I understand if you don't want to work for me anymore—"

"Are you kidding? Of course I want to still work for you!"

"You do? But what if my company doesn't grow beyond where it is now?"

"It will," Juliet said with perfect certainty. "You've created such a strong brand that people are more than willing to come to you now, like the reporters did. We'll just block out some filming time, and since you seem to prefer filming on the road, I'll bet it will actually be pretty easy."

Easy. Could it really be easy?

Although, even as she asked herself the question, she suddenly realized that the hard part wasn't actually *doing* it. The hard part was *believing* that she could do it...and working out exactly what it was that she wanted.

Finally, Morgan knew for sure what that was: She wanted to go back to Walker Island. And she wanted Brian.

Forever.

CHAPTER TWENTY

Football practice was not going well. In fact, it was fair to say that it was the worst it had gone all summer. The kids were enthusiastic enough, but they had an entire playbook to work through, new players to integrate, and a coach who had other things on his mind. Brian focused just long enough to watch the play in front of him, then sighed and blew his whistle.

"Run it again, and do it right this time."

"But Coach," one of them said, "we've already run it five times!"

Brian's immediate reaction was to tell the kid to drop and do a hundred push-ups for talking back, but he stopped before he could say it. Even the fact that he'd thought it was bad enough...especially when he checked his copy of the playbook and realized he hadn't even been looking at the right play.

"You're right, Timmy. You've run it enough times for today. Let's take a quick water break."

How could he not have been looking at the right play? He'd written it. He should have known the details without even having to look.

But Brian already knew the answer: He'd been thinking about Morgan. Asking himself for the thousandth time if he'd been wrong to let her go. All night long he'd gone over and over the possible scenarios, but each time he came to the same place—if he'd pressured her to stay when she didn't truly want to, she would have ended up resenting him. And no amount of love in the world would make up for that bitterness.

Still, it took every ounce of self-control he possessed not to just abandon practice, rush down to the docks, head over to the airport, and book a ticket to New York so that he could somehow persuade her to come back to him.

He'd really thought that this time she might actually want to stay. That they might be able to find a way to make it work. And that she might not need to be on the opposite coast to be who she really was. Yet, apparently, the seven years that had gone by just meant more responsibilities for her. More reasons they couldn't be together.

Brian forced himself to snap out of it and blew his whistle again, intending to start the football team off on some tackling drills. But instead of getting ready for the drill he called out, they went over to form a line at one side of the field, Tad at their head, while Natalie watched intently from the stands. At least *one* of them had gotten the girl. What's more, Brian had been surprised to learn that Morgan had sent Natalie a list of universities that had forward-thinking science departments *and* strong football teams.

"What are you doing?" Brian asked. "This isn't the formation for the drill."

Brian blew his whistle again for emphasis, but it was drowned out by the blare of a trumpet a beat before the school's band marched onto the football field in full uniform, as if they were ready for a big show.

"What's going on?" Brian shouted over the music. "Where's your band leader? There's been a mistake. The football team has the field booked."

But they didn't stop playing, and suddenly, he realized that they weren't playing one of their usual tunes. Instead, they were playing *You and Me*, the same song that had been playing when Brian had kissed Morgan at the prom. The football players seemed to be in on it, too, as they formed up with the rest of the band, Tad directing them a little awkwardly, but still managing to keep everyone on beat.

Brian couldn't believe what he was hearing as the familiar, sweet notes were reinterpreted for a marching band complete with tuba. It shouldn't have even come close to working, yet the sheer poignancy of the moment overrode the rest of it as the band began to create several concentric circles while the football players hung around the edges. But all of them were looking at one person standing in the middle of the field.

Morgan.

She was wearing a dress almost exactly like the prom dress she had worn all those years ago and had a garland of wild flowers in her hair. For a moment, it was like going back in time.

The thought had barely passed through his mind when he realized that they didn't need to go back to the past. Not when Morgan was even more beautiful now than she had been back then. Not when they were both a lot older and wiser.

And not when Brian loved her more than he ever had.

He started running across the field, as fast as he could to get to her. And yet, it still took far too long to weave through the lines of the marching band and finally pull her into his arms.

Brian kissed her then, deeply and passionately, ignoring the cheers from the band and football players around them. Her garland was a little crooked by the time they finally drew back from each other, but she looked as beautiful as ever. Although, he suddenly realized, there was one thing about her that was different—she wasn't wearing makeup.

She looked as beautiful without it as she ever did with it, but Brian still understood how huge this was for her. To be without the perfect mask, just for once, so that she could show him the real her with nothing else between them.

"I wanted to make a really big gesture to apologize for running off on you again. And to convince you to forgive me."

"You never have to apologize to me, Morgan. And there's nothing to forgive. There never was. I've always loved you, through thick and thin, near and far. Although," he said as he dipped his mouth down to press it against hers again, "I'm hoping this is your way of telling me you want to be *near*."

"I do," she confirmed with another kiss of her own, before adding, "But I also really wanted to do something big to show you how much I love you."

"I've always known that you love me, just as much as I love you," he told her. "But I'm still impressed that you managed to do all this."

Morgan smiled, saying, "I'm a Walker," and for the first time, she sounded truly pleased about it. "This is my great-grandfather's island. My grandfather built the school. I grew up surrounded by the most incredible people. Especially you, Brian." In her eyes, he saw a brighter spark of passion and joy than he ever had before. "This is where I belong. With you and my family."

"But do you really think you can run your career from here without feeling you had to give up everything that you've worked so hard for and that matters so much to you?" God, he hated having to ask, but if he didn't, he'd wonder forever if he'd let her make the wrong decision. "Because you deserve to have it all, Morgan, and I would never want to be in your way."

"I'm going to figure out how to do it all from here," Morgan vowed. "The garden was a start, and hopefully you'll be able to take some time off now and again to come with me on the road as I film my traveling makeover segments. Plus, I was thinking during the taxi ride and on the ferry back to the island that it might not be that difficult to convince my sister Hanna to set up a studio for both of us here. After the way every one of the reporters I invited came, I now know people will travel to the island to work and film. Not just because they want to work with me, but also because Walker Island is somewhere people can't resist visiting. It's a magical place that's always been full of dreams. And love. So much love that I can't imagine ever living anywhere else. Just as I can't imagine living with *anyone* else. There's no other love for me, Brian. Only you. *Always* you."

Brian couldn't wait another moment to go down on one knee, right there in the mud of the football field. "Marry me, Morgan, and make me the happiest man alive."

Her *yes* was drowned out by the cheers of the football players and band members.

EPILOGUE

Rachel looked over the happy chaos of Morgan and Brian's new home, not far from the Walker house, with its view over the waterfront and its small garden, already full of aromatic plants. There were still moving boxes everywhere, but Morgan clearly was far more interested in putting the finishing touches on the makeovers of a couple of high school girls in her makeshift studio than she was with finishing her unpacking. Hanna was moving around the studio with a handheld video camera so that she could shoot Morgan and the teenagers with the backdrop of the ocean behind them.

Automatically, Rachel slipped into mentally working out the risks the way she did every day at the insurance firm she worked for. She tried not to wince at the thought of all the accidents caused each year by trailing wires when she knew she should be simply enjoying having Morgan and Hanna home again, instead.

Morgan had changed the entire feel of her new show to real people getting real makeovers in their hometowns. She was no longer focused on glitz and perfection, but on showing people just how beautiful they already were. And based on the viewer reaction and enthusiasm from the pilot Hanna had helped Morgan shoot, the show was a hit.

Rachel was so proud of her sisters. They were both so talented, and they'd worked so hard. Working in insurance, Rachel knew all about long odds. It was amazing—and incredibly gratifying—that two of her sisters had beaten them. They deserved all the success that they got and more.

Charlotte tugged on her hand. "Mommy, I want to play dress-up with Aunt Morgan and her makeup."

"As soon as she's done filming, I'm sure she'd love to play with you," Rachel whispered to her daughter. Morgan always had time for her little niece, no matter how long and busy her workdays were, and it made Rachel love her sister even more.

The wind had picked up as Hanna moved one of her cameras outside, and just as she turned her back on the heavy camera and stand, it started to tumble. Thankfully, Joel was there like a shot, catching it and setting it back on its tripod, taking the opportunity to kiss his wife once everything was safely back into place. Brian was there, too, as he'd been carrying bites of French toast to Morgan between shots.

"Everything looks like it's going great," Michael said as he came out of the house, where he was helping with some repairs. Emily was only a few steps behind him, looking as pleased as the rest of them and carrying a plate of fragrant cinnamon buns that she'd been making in the nearby kitchen for the cast and crew.

Paige snagged one as she finally arrived from the dance studio and sat down under the shade of an oak tree to watch the filming. "Thanks, Em. I haven't eaten since early this morning. Isn't this amazing what Morgan and Hanna are doing?"

It really was amazing, Rachel thought, having her sisters all in one place again and knowing that they were happy. One day soon, all of the Walker sisters would be paired up the way Morgan and Hanna were with men they loved. Everyone but her.

And she was fine with that. She really was. She didn't need anybody else. *They* didn't need anybody else. After Charlotte's father had left, Rachel had vowed never to let another man get close enough to hurt either of them again. Her precious daughter was better off without someone in her life who would only walk away once things got tough. They both were.

Which was why, instead of focusing on what

she would never have, Rachel would always remember how she'd been lucky enough to beat the odds by having the most beautiful daughter, family and place to live in the entire world.

~ THE END ~

ABOUT THE AUTHOR

When New York Times and USA Today bestseller Lucy Kevin released her first novel, SEATTLE GIRL, it became an instant bestseller. All of her subsequent sweet contemporary romances have been hits with readers as well, including WHEN IT'S LOVE (A Walker Island Romance, Book 3) which debuted at #1. Having been called "One of the top writers in America" by The Washington Post, she recently launched the very romantic Walker Island series. Lucy also writes contemporary romances as Bella Andre and her incredibly popular series about The Sullivans have been #1 bestsellers around the world, with more than 4 million books sold so far! If not behind her computer, you can find her swimming, hiking or laughing with her husband and two children. www.LucyKevin.com

Printed in Great Britain
by Amazon.co.uk, Ltd.,
Marston Gate.